MW01136530

AT THE END OF ALL THINGS

A novella by

Frank Reteguiz

Amazon Edition

ataboolife@gmail.com

ISBN: 9781090233783

"At the end of all things there is and shall always be . . ."

Introduction: A Constant Wanderer

I am a constant wanderer.

Never fitting in.

Ever lonely but accepting who I am.

Searching for, I forget what.

I have lived many lives.

I have traveled many miles.

Many stories I have.

For you, I will tell them.

The Descent

It felt like a good day to do the necessary, and I'd picked the spot I wanted to see one last time.

I'd stayed the night at the Monte Vista Hotel, my favorite hotel of all my travels. I'd spent the night at a restaurant down the street, eating the best bacon cheeseburger I'd ever had, and then I'd followed it up with a liquid dessert that consisted of gin and tonics and Old Fashioneds, my favorites. Surprisingly, I hadn't woken up with a hangover. Instead, rays of light from the rising sun warmed my face as I woke from my plush, comfortable bed.

I walked through the noir-style hotel room and opened my window. The cold Flagstaff mountain air caressed my face as I looked onto the streets of the quaint town. It was quiet and the streets were empty, except for the restaurant. I was pleased I'd chosen to see this place one last time. It was one of my favorite towns to visit. Even though I wasn't planning on sleeping in the room again, I'd paid for one last night, so I left my luggage and my teddy bear, which I'd had since childhood. I wasn't going to need any of those anymore, but I didn't want to bring them with me. I wanted to leave my belongings in that room because that was the last place that felt like home. As I left my room, I looked back and felt sorrow seeing the teddy bear on the bed, leaning on its side and looking toward me, as if it were sad to see me leave.

The drive to the canyon was gorgeous. It was less than two hours, but I drove through green forest with fields of bright yellow daisies that changed to desert as the elevation increased. At the front gates of the Grand Canyon, I paid for a day pass. I parked my black 1967 Mustang in the parking lot and left my cell phone in the glove compartment. I retrieved a pen and recorded the make and model of my car, the license plate number, and the address of the hotel on a sheet of paper. Then I placed the paper into my wallet to ensure it would be found later, locked the car, walked a few feet, and turned around so that I could admire the Mustang, the car I'd always wanted. I was glad I bought and fixed my dream car. It took me a year to fix her, but she was worth it. She took me to places I needed to be. It was sad leaving her there by herself.

The trolley ride to the trailhead was peaceful. I was alone on the trolley as it was the off-season for tourists, which was good because I didn't want children coming across what I was about to do. Plus, I didn't want to be stopped by some Good Samaritan.

After the trolley dropped me off, I walked to the gift shop and bought a sports drink and bottle of water. I just needed enough electrolytes and water to get me to my intended spot. I chugged the energy drink and threw it in the trash, then *stored the bottle of water in my cargo pants pocket.*

I walked to edge of the trail and marveled at Grand Canyon's beauty. I'd always said that pictures could never do the canyon justice; it had to be seen for oneself. I looked out into the canyon's awe-inspiring vastness. Who knew wear and tear could make something so beautiful?

The time on my black Fossil watch read nearly 8:00 a.m. I estimated the hike would take four hours to travel five miles. I took one last look of the entire canyon and then started my way.

The hike was easy, since I was working with gravity. By the time I reached the three-mile mark, I'd seen only twenty hikers, the last one an hour ago.

I stared down into the canyon, where I could see my final destination. Another hour to get there. The morning's temperature had been a wonderful 72 degrees, but now it felt like a 100. The sun was starting to burn my forehead as I kept hiking to my destination. I chugged the last of my water and placed the empty bottle back into my pocket. Strange how I still cared about littering.

I estimated another 200 yards to go as I walked to my spot. I glanced at my watch again. It was nearing 1:30 p.m. The hike had taken longer than I'd imagined. I trembled as I made my final steps to my destination. I was both frightened and relieved about what would happen next. The life I had would never be the same. Circumstances unseen chose me, but I was the one who'd made the decision.

I walked to the edge of the canyon and sat on the cliff. It was quietly pleasant and serene. The only tourists in visual range were the ones rafting on the Colorado River, about one thousand feet below me. I sat there for what seemed like hours, sitting at the center of the most beautiful place on earth. I sat there by the beautiful imagery, engulfed by the colors of time painted on the canyon walls. Looking west, I saw nothing but clear skies. To the east, dark clouds formed in the distance. The muffled sound of thunder echoed in the canyon. I didn't want a storm to ruin this day. I'd already had too many storms ruin my life.

I took one last look at the place in which I'd come to find peace, then pulled out my wallet and confirmed the paper with the hotel and my car information was still there. I looked at my license and read my name aloud, "Rick Esperanza." I wanted to forget that name.

I placed my wallet back into its original pocket, then reached into my cargo pants pocket and took out my gun. I was surprised nobody had noticed the clunky bulge in my pocket, not even the park rangers. Given today's age of school, mall, and movie theater shootings, the rangers seemed complacent, or maybe they weren't used to looking for people with guns.

I held the Glock 30 in my hands, staring at it. I'd loaded the weapon with eleven .45 caliber hollow point rounds, but I only needed one.

I felt indifferent at this point. I thought I'd try to talk myself out of it or be more fearful. Even though I'd been taught through my Catholic upbringing that what I was doing was the worst of all sins, a spit in God's face, I just didn't care anymore. Tired and empty, I was done with this world. My life was over long before I made the trip to the canyon.

I thought this would be the part when a miracle would happen, but I sat there in silence the only sound the wind flowing through the canyon. I looked to the east one last time and watched the storm clouds growing larger, drifting my direction. I looked to the west. Nothing but sunshine and clear skies over the Colorado River. I kept my gaze west as I placed the barrel against my temple and my finger on the trigger. I wanted the last image to be a beautiful ending and not another storm. Slowly, I pulled the trigger, my eyes westward. I was glad I'd seen the canyon one last time. My eyes closed involuntarily as I gently squeezed the trigger.

"Please save me," I pleaded to the unknown.

The Ascent

An explosive thunder echoed across the majestic walls.

Rick opened his eyes. Through his tears, the blackness slowly turned into obscured light. Eyes wide open he stared in shock at the Grand Canyon.

Did I succeed? Am I dead? Is this Purgatory? Perdition? Paradise?

Rick felt the weight of the Glock in his hand, still pressed against his temple. Slowly, he brought it to his lap and starred at the ugly black pistol for what felt like hours. He was afraid to check but he had to know. Slowly grasping the slide and gently pulling it to its rear, he ejected the bullet from the chamber and onto his lap. His stomach turned as he realized the bullet had not fired.

Did I pull the trigger?

He knew he'd squeezed the trigger. He'd heard an explosion. Slowly, nervously he raised the bullet from his lap. Bringing the rear of the bullet into his sight, his stomach cringed with pain from the impending revelation. The imprint of the firing pin was on the primer; the bullet should have fired.

An explosion boomed through the Canyon. Quickly, he turned his head and realized the explosion was only thunder echoing through the canyon walls, sounds from the distant storm.

His eyes darted back to the bullet's primer. He stared briefly, then heartache and confusion overwhelmed him. His stomach ached. His body went weak with shame and sadness as he dry heaved into the canyon. Rick threw the Glock and watched as it slowly spun, falling through the air and splashing into the Colorado River. His body fell limp as he curled into the fetal position, squeezing the bullet in his palm. Tears of hysteria streamed from his face as the pain in his stomach became unbearable from the realization that he was still alive.

"Why?" he moaned. "Why didn't it fire?" Rick cried into the empty desert air, "WHY AM I STILL ALIVE?" The shock overcame him, and he passed out onto the spot that was to be his resting space.

* * *

"Wake up," she said, poking his chest. Rick moaned and went back to sleep. "Wake up," she said gently, poking his chest with more pressure.

Rick slowly opened his eyes and gazed at the silhouette of a woman standing over him, the glaring sun above her. He squinted as she slowly came into focus. Even after this strenuous event, he could not help his heart racing at the sight of her. His gaze started from her dust-covered hiking boots up to her curvy, but firm, legs, accentuated through her worn blue jeans. She wore a brown and white flannel shirt, the front shirttails tied in a bow, her midriff covered by a white camisole. Rick looked past her voluptuous body, taken aback by her face. If this were paradise, then she would be an angel, and if this were perdition, then she would be his torture, the last heavenly thing he'd ever see. Her auburn hair flowed with the breeze, blocking the sun enough for him to see her face. Her smile, brighter and warmer than the sun, was a smile of relief, and her eyes nearly stopped his heart. Hazel eyes deep and stark. She wasn't looking at Rick. She was looking through him with a look of deep concern.

"Hello, Rick," she gently said. "You need to get up. We have a long hike, and there's a lot we have to talk about."

"Who are you, and how do you know who I am?" Rick demanded, standing slowly from the cliff and slyly pocketing the bullet.

"Me?" she said with a smile. "Don't worry about that; that's not important now. As for how I know your name, I have always known it. . . ."

She trailed off at the exact moment the look of disbelief overtook Rick's face. A cold chill passed through his spine as he started to back away from her.

"You should stop, Rick. I don't want you to walk off the cliff and actually finish what you've started."

Rick stopped in shock and disbelief. "Who the fuck are you?" he screamed. "Why are you following me!"

"Rick, Rick, Rick," she said, seemly undeterred by his rage. "Let's start hiking, and I'll explain everything. But we need to leave now because you're working against the clock."

"The clock?"

"A storm is coming. The one you see in the east. It's going to be pretty bad once it gets here, and since you didn't bring any water or anything with electrolytes, your body is going to give out on you probably before we make it back." She smiled coyly. "You might get your wish after all."

"I'm not leaving until you tell me why you're here," Rick asserted.

"I was sent here. You have somebody interested in your welfare."

"Who sent you?"

"That's not important. What's important is that you trust me and listen to what I have to say."

"Trust you? Who the fuck *are* you? Why are you stalking me? And stop talking in fucking riddles!"

The woman stood underneath the sweltering sun, never wavering or distressing. Her stare was calm and compassionate. "Rick, I was sent here because you needed help. I know who you are because I have a special interest in you. As for me, I'm your companion for the journey back."

Rick hesitated, then asked, "Am I dead?"

"What do you think?" she playfully asked. "That bullet in your pocket is evidence that the worst decision you ever made was a failure."

Rick shivered. "You're scaring me. How do you know so much?"

"Let's go." Her tone was sweet but commanding. "We need to start our hike back. We've a lot to discuss."

Moments of silence passed as they stared into each other's eyes.

What is this? Rick thought. *Is this a hallucination? Is this a symptom of dehydration, or did I finally lose touch with reality?*

Despite his fear, Rick stared into her eyes. It was those hazel eyes that finally convinced him to trust her.

He stepped toward her, shaking his head.

She grinned ear to ear as she wrapped both arms around his arm and said, "Let's get going." Then she whispered into his ear as they began the trek back to the top, "I am not a hallucination."

5 Miles

"Tell me who you think I am," she said as they walked through the flat valley.

Rick hiked quietly for a few moments as he formulated his words. "I have two prevailing thoughts on that. The first is a creepy thought; that you're a stalker who went to great lengths to follow me."

She asked, "Then how did I know about the bullet in your pocket?"

"You could be just observant and noticed me putting it in my pocket. You would have known the bullet didn't fire because you saw me pull the trigger, and then you saw me unload it into my lap."

She smiled. "Good guess but wrong, sweetie. What's your second hypothesis?"

"You do not exist. You're a figment of my imagination. You're a symptom of my psychosis, produced from the stress and trauma I endured. Instead of having PTSD, I ended up with schizophrenia."

"Oh Rick. My intelligent Rick, I always loved that about you. You look for logic. Always trying to rationalize and deduce. But you're wrong. I am real." She nudged him playfully. "Don't I feel real?"

"Bullshit!" Rick yelled, stumbling over a rock. "Who the fuck are you?"

She helped him to his feet. "I told you my name is not important. Who sent me and what I am will be explained later. The important thing is why I'm here."

"OK, why are you here?"

"I'm here to help you, and to do that, I need to tell you some stories."

Rick glared at her. "Stories? Help me with what? My miserable life?" Rick asked as they hiked toward the empty campsites at the checkpoint for the canyon path.

"No, to help you see that you have a meaning in life and that your suffering has a role in it," she answered, gracefully hiking over a step.

"This sounds Shakespearian. No, I take that back. This sounds like something from *It's a Wonderful Life* but without the family to run home to or the happy ending. Unless you want to go behind that boulder over there and give me a happy ending?" Rick flirted.

She went quiet for a brief moment as she continued to hike besides him. He wondered why she wasn't sweating in this sweltering heat, but he did notice her cheeks slightly blush.

"That's not going to work on me or any woman for that matter, and I know you're better than that. That womanizing front you put on is really a self-defense mechanism you use to disguise your pain and your fear of rejection. You would rather have people think you're a misogynist than let them see your kind heart and feel vulnerable."

She tugged on his arm, signaling for Rick to stop and look her in the eye. "When you act like a womanizer, that's when you're at your weakest because you're letting people think you're less then what you really are." Rick tried to find the words to defend himself, but it was futile against the truth. "You're also wrong about the *It's a Wonderful Life* and the Shakespearian analogy. I see myself as Virgil. Now come along, Dante. I have stories to tell." She flashed a reassuring smile and then hiked ahead of him.

Rick hesitated briefly, considering perhaps she was right.

"Here is the story of a good man," she began.

The Rōnin's Story

"There are no heroes in the world, and if there are, then I am not one of them," said the weary man to himself. He sat at the bar on a dark and stormy night, and his face told the story of a young man's face made older through horrors untold. The man wore an expensive suit, though he seemed uncomfortable in it. He looked as if being in a uniform or some official garb might be more preferable to him. His watch said a man of class, but the scars on his fists and face said he was a man who came from a different walk of life, a man who knew darkness, unlike the other expensively clad men at the bar.

"I used to be a protector of men, something I was proud to do; but it's gone because I couldn't look the other way." He pitied himself as he took another drink of scotch. "Two years ago I was doing something I loved and took pride in, but I couldn't look the other way, and now I can never go back to that life."

He sipped his scotch, enjoying the strength from its age. The weary man looked up from his drink and past the top-shelf spirits, watching the dark reflection of himself, then shamefully looking away. "I miss it. I miss the chase. I miss the thrill. I miss the chills down my spine. I was good at what I did and I loved it. It was a lonely life and I cursed it sometimes, but I knew who I was when I did it. I felt honorable. But now I can't even look at myself."

Across the bar, a pretty blonde seemed uncomfortable with a slick-looking yuppie, persisting with sad and desperate attempts to get her into bed.

"Why did I survive? Maybe I should have died. There are things worse than death, like losing your purpose for living. Now I live in pain and regret. My body aches from wear and tear, from battles old. My knees throb from the miles I've trod. My lower back and shoulders hurt from the fights. It hurts to breath sometimes. The old scars on my fists and face are reminders of my brutal life. But, it's my heart that hurts most of all, for it misses the good it once did."

He signaled the bartender for another scotch. "Why couldn't I look the other way? Why couldn't I have been like everyone else and just went with it?" He gulped the expensive scotch, then placed the glass to his temple to ease a spasm. "I did what I did because I couldn't look the other way. I couldn't stand by and do nothing. There were men who had more power than I had who could have stopped or even prevented the corruption from happening, but they chose to look the other way because they were afraid. They were afraid to lose the life they were comfortable with, even if it came at a cost to the innocent. I did what I did because somebody had to, but it cost me the career I loved. . . . Fuck, maybe I did it because I was obsessed and couldn't accept losing. Maybe I'm not a hero. Maybe I did it because I had an ego and couldn't let it down." He sipped again and wiped a tear from his eye.

"Nobody ever tells you that when you go down the path of doing the right thing that you'll walk alone," he continued. "Nobody tells you how hard it is. I don't even know if it made a difference, if my actions actually meant something. I lost it all, and it took two years to rebuild my life to the point where I have more money, fancy clothes, and cars than I had before, but what's the point if there's no meaning to it? If there's no reason to fight?"

The yuppie pulled aggressively on the blonde's arm as she tried pulling away. Desperately, she searched for someone to help her, but everyone looked the other way. She yelled for the bartender, but he turned his back on her to wash wine glasses. The weary man noticed the familiar bulge of a pistol underneath the yuppie's Gucci coat.

She looked to him and cried for help, but the weary man looked away, disgusted with himself for doing so. "I have to fit in. I can't go back to that life. I can't. If I do then I'll lose everything. It will kill me if I go back to who I was."

The woman screamed for help as the yuppie dragged her off her stool and toward the rear exit of the bar. The rich and powerful came to this bar, but they either ignored her pleas or mocked them in a cruel attempt to be witty. His heart raced in his chest as he felt a surge of energy course through his body. His awareness sharpened as the hairs on the back of his neck become sensitive to the softest flow of air. His fist clenched and his feet slowly turned to the scream. "No. No. No! Not anymore," he told himself. "I can't do this anymore. I can't . . ."

"Oh, God! Please somebody help me!" the woman screamed for her life.

He broke the rock glass in his hands. The bar went quiet and stared at him. Blood flowed from his hand, but he felt no pain; the aches and pains across his body seized as his blood burned hot and his muscles tensed. His stool flew back as he charged out the bar, knocking over the indifferent, the cruel, and the cowardly in his path. He felt alive again. He could no longer deny who he was.

"This may be my last battle. I may lose it all, but at least I will have my soul back," said the rōnin as he went forth into darkness for one last fight.

* * *

Rick hiked on quietly after hearing the tale of the rōnin. "Why did you just—"

She cut him off from asking his question with a question of her own. "Why did you want to commit suicide?"

Rick walked quietly for a few moments, shamefully considering his answer. "Don't you know why? You said you knew so much about me."

"I need to hear it from your mouth. You need to say it out loud and not let it rot inside you as you've been doing."

Rick became even more uneasy around her. He thought about running away, but how do you run away from your own insanity?

"Like the rōnin said, 'I'm no hero. I did something not a lot of people would have done, and I am not sure if I was right for doing it. I lost the things I love because of it.'"

She lovingly assured him, "You are and you did, but you need to tell me your story. Not for my sake but for yours."

Rick found a stone the size of a bowling ball and furiously flung it to the east.

"Are you here to taunt me? Are you here to remind me why I should die? I just want to be at peace! I want to die!" Rick yelled, turning away from his companion to hide his tears.

The caring woman walked in front of him and gently grabbed his hands. He lifted his face, and her warm hazel eyes met his, easing his overwhelming despair.

A loud explosion sounded in the distance. His gaze broke from her loving eyes, and he noticed the gray clouds in the east growing larger and darker.

"We need to keep going," she said. "I don't have much time with you and you need to hear my stories."

Rick collected himself and wiped his. He was an imposing man. His size caused terror in others, even with a minor outburst. But not her, for she calmed the misunderstood beast with her kindness and compassion. Gently, she tugged on his hand. He followed her back to the trail.

4 Miles

"Why do I need to hear these stories?" He breathed heavier as the trail became steeper.

She cheerfully answered without missing a breath, "Each of these stories has a purpose, as we all have a purpose. Some of them might seem fantastical, but they all have a meaning; they all have a part to play. Just as your story does, when you're ready to tell it."

"Is the message from the story of rōnin about chivalry? About defending the honor of a damsel in distress?" he asked cynically.

"No . . . wait. Well, some of it was." she said, her voice bright and bubbly. "It's about being true to who you are. The rōnin represents a good part of you, a good part in all of us, as long as we don't deny it. We all have the ability to be brave; we just have to choose to be. You know you're a good man, but you deny it. You deny it for the same reason he did; he couldn't accept it until life forced himself to see it. And you will see it too at the end of our journey."

"I'm not a hero. I don't even know why I did what I did back in Savannah." Rick stops himself from remembering the pain. "What's the point of being a good person, a courageous person, if evil wins? Fuck, I tried to fight it back in . . ." Rick stopped and stared into the distance as his tormented memories came back. He used some breathing techniques he'd learned to help stop the overwhelming emotions, and then calmly he said, "The corrupt, the cheaters, and the liars always win. There is no karma. There is no poetic justice. Evil wins because they don't play by the rules."

"No, if good people like you don't get them, then their own sins do. The universe always balances itself out," she said as they hiked on the steeper grade of the trail.

Monstrous Me

"I've done evil things that I quite enjoyed," the well-dressed man said to himself, walking the narrow alley of Pikes Place Market. His step had a gleeful hop as he walked down the alley in the cold and drizzle. "Bad men pay me to do the things they cannot do because they fear losing their already tarnished soul. If the devil existed, then he would cringe for the things I do for the right price," said the well-dressed man, taking a whiff of the coffee and the wet, salty air.

"If those fools only knew that hearing a man scream, a woman beg, and child cry is payment enough for my deeds. While others embrace compassion and good will with righteous might, I embrace evil with all its lovely delights." The well-dressed man danced in the moonlight of the cold and dreary night, until he stopped and spied an alley door slightly ajar. "I have stolen fortunes, I have stolen retirements, and I have stolen futures; why not steal a little more?" The well-dressed man slid elegantly through the opening, as nimble as a ballerina.

Thud! The door shut behind him, but he did not startle, because he was fear in the flesh. The well-dressed man checked the door and found it locked. "Oh, no matter. I didn't see an alarm box on the outside. Maybe there'll be some expensive gifts on the way out."

The well-dressed man took a step forward and stopped, for something caught the corner of his eye. He looked down the pitch-black hallway of the business and tried adjusting his eyes to the dark. The drizzle turned to hard rain and thunder, but the man heard something else. He waited and listened and heard somebody breathing at the hall's end. Like the predator he was, he stood and waited as he prepared his attack. Slowly he reached in his coat pocket and retrieved a dagger, sharper than sin.

The well-dressed man took a step forward and saw a black silhouette grow at the end of the hallway. His heart raced as he strained to see its face. The man had learned through his career how to sneak up on someone without making a sound; each foot touched the ground gently as he moved closer to the creature at the end of the hall. The figure moved too as the well-dressed man moved closer. He began to ponder what was wrong, for his heart raced. He had never felt fear before. His eyes adjusted, and he could see minor details of the creature at the end of the hall. It was taller and wider than him with buck-like horns. The well-dressed man watched the creature staring back, noting the dull gleam of its fangs.

The thunder grew louder as the well-dressed man began to panic. "No!" he yelled. "I have killed many men. Some were big and vicious and others were brave, but all met the same fate with the dagger in my hand." He threatened the creature at the end of the hall.

As his eyes adjusted, he made out fur that draped off the creature's shoulders and eyes that glowed blood red. The well-dressed man had met his demon, and he attended to kill him like the rest. The well-dressed man ran forward, his dagger raised high, ready to gut the creature, but to his terrifying surprise, the creature ran toward him too, its sharp claw raised in ready for the attack. For the first time, the man felt dread as he made his desperate advance. The man leapt forward at the creature and swung his dagger down onto its head.

Glass shattered, and the well-dressed man lay on the ground, large shards of glass piercing his body. The man expected another attack and quickly reached for his dagger but could not grasp it for the shard of glass impaling his wrist. A bolt of lightning struck nearby, illuminating the night as if it were day.

The man looked up at his monster, a mounted buck's head above a vanity mirror, a fur coat hanging off its posts; the humming of an oscillating fan next to the mirror was the imaginary creature's breath. The man laughed hysterically . . . and then cried at the sight of the large piece of glass protruding through his leg. Blood poured from his femoral artery. There was no way he would make it out alive.

As he lay there staring into the reflection of the broken vanity mirror, he saw himself bloodied and mutilated, broken glass across his body. Fearing for what came next, the room growing black again, he whispered over his last breath, "I am the monster."

* * *

"So what's the metaphor? Evil never wins out?" Rick asked, smacking his severely parched lips.

"No, evil is always destructive, to the point of self-destruction. At some point, evil will kill itself, but before that happens, it destroys everything before its end. This is why good people are needed, to stop the destruction before it can hurt the innocent."

"I'm not a good person. I've been called selfish, arrogant . . . now I'm mentally unstable. Why would a good person have any of these characteristics?"

"Nobody is perfect. Hell, Martin Luther King Jr. was an adulterer, and he tried to commit suicide twice, but he still changed the world. You don't have to be a saint to do what is good; you just have to do it."

3 Miles

The storm in the east gradually stalked its way west, growing fiercer and darker. Anything that was once bright and full of life was now gray and sickly underneath the shadow of the growing storm. The storm was Death and it was coming for Rick.

* * *

Rick and his unknown companion continued their hike as they began taking higher strides up the steeper ascent. They stopped at a wooden rest shack at the three-mile checkpoint. The resting spot provided a water refill station. Rick ran to the faucet and eagerly turned the sprocket so that he could quench his parched mouth. He put his lips over the faucet and waited for a minute until just a drop of water fell on his tongue.

"What the fuck?" he screamed, kicking at the pipes. His companion perched herself against the rustic wall of the shack and looked to the east, unfazed by Rick's rant. For the first time since the hike, Rick watched as his companion had no longer a cheerful and calm demeanor but now donned a mournful expression, a look of doom.

"Hey, stranger," Rick said in a warm and nurturing tone. "What are you worried about?"

She didn't answer but kept staring into the approaching monstrous storm.

Rick perched himself next to her, close enough to smell her lovely musk and feel her smooth skin brush against his arm. He stared at the storm with her, the chills traveling down his spine, as he finally understood her feeling of doom. Even though it was still in the distance, the storm looked like a biblical plague about to be unleashed on the Grand Canyon.

She looked into the menacing storm, letting a few more moments of silence pass. "We don't have much time left." She turned her gaze toward him and smiled assuredly. It was the sort of smile a medic would give while lying to a dying soldier. "It's going to be all right," she said.

Rick knew that smile all too well. He'd given it himself and received it too many times.

He reached for her hand, and for the first time in a long time, offered a genuine smile. "It's going to be OK. We're going to get out of this. I'm going to get you to shelter before the storm hits."

She turned to him and smiled widely. "There's the real you: the protector, the leader, the one who cares." She pulled at his hand, and they continued hiking. "I have a story to tell you about the part of yourself you just displayed," she said, "and conveniently it's about a vicious storm."

The Final Voyage of the USS *Maelstrom*

I had joined the navy when I was a young man filled with blind ambition. I had dreams of seeing the world and embarking on adventures while searching for inspiration to become the next great novelist. While stationed in the Public Affairs Office in Virginia, I was issued the fateful orders; I was to cover the retirement of Captain Leroy Santos and the decommissioning of his warship, the USS *Maelstrom*.

Every sailor, from any country, has heard of the legend of Captain Santos and the *Maelstrom*. His ship had taken on the most impossible missions in the Great War: outmaneuvering the fastest enemy ships, sinking battleships with twice the firepower than the *Maelstrom*, and successfully capturing five U-boats from three different missions. But, it was the Battle of Gibraltar — or what the public knows as the Miracle at Gibraltar — that made him a myth. The *Maelstrom* patrolled the crucial strait under attacked by a fleet of six enemy ships trying to gun their way through to take control of the strait. Most other captains would have retreated and waited for reinforcements; but no, not Captain Santos, he raged forth with the USS *Maelstrom*. The old warship not only held off the advancing fleet but also sank the two battleships in its group while critically damaging the three frigates while the remaining frigate retreated. Captain Santos had become the most decorated sailor in the US Navy with that battle, now taught and studied in naval colleges across the world. My granddad once told me as a child that there are two types of people who can make miracles happen in the world: saints and mad men. Captain Santos was no saint.

It had been twenty years since the end of the Great War, and the Admiralty could no longer justify funding the deteriorating warship. She was to take her final voyage to Charlestown Naval Yard where she was to be mothballed and become a floating museum. The captain, on the other hand, had been offered the rank of admiral every year for the past fifteen, but he refused to leave the helm of the *Maelstrom*. Now he was entering retirement involuntarily. My assignment was to board the *Maelstrom* and document its final voyage for the museum.

The following night, I was in Kings Bay Naval Base being taxied to the pier where the *Maelstrom* was docked. In my imagination, I envisioned the *Maelstrom* as a freshly painted, massive, and formidable ship of war that would make the enemy shit their pants, but instead I witnessed a shell of her former self. Once majestic but now battle weary, her hull was covered with rust. I was sad to see her poor patch jobs of old shell damage and to hear her engine clanking and choking on its last breaths. I tried to show respect and admiration to the warship, but all I could feel was pity. She needed to be put out of her misery. I waited in line at the gangway behind other members of the press, admirals, and a senator waiting to board the old warship to take part in the final voyage. The ship's crew stood in formation on the mooring deck in their dress whites as the executive officer — Captain Santos nowhere in sight — stood in front and gave the order of presenting arms as we boarded the ship. After settling into the crew quarters, made hospitable to the best of the crew's abilities, we all stood on the weather deck and watched the USS *Maelstrom* disembark from Kings Bay to take her final voyage.

I spent the better part of the day taking tours and interviewing crewmembers, but to my disappointment, I did not seen Captain Santos. I was given a chance to interview the XO after he made his rounds on the ship. He was close to retirement himself, as he was one of the last original crew of the *Maelstrom*. The jovial XO entertained me with a firsthand account of the stories of the *Maelstrom* and the now mysterious Captain Santos. He had been just a scared shitless ensign during the Battle of Gibraltar, not knowing if he'd make it past that night, but Captain Santos had a hypnotic effect on the crew. Somehow during the hellish fight, where brave men cried in fear, he had commanded their courage and had gotten the crew to forget about dying and focus on bringing hell to the enemy. I asked him why we hadn't met with the great captain, at which he point his face shifted from joyful nostalgia to disappointment. He said that the captain hadn't been himself since the news of his forced retirement and since having his ship commandeered. The navy was the captain's life. He was an old salty dog harden by war who could do anything as long as he was with his *Maelstrom*; now, however, he was being told never to sail the seas, as was his purpose.

Since having received the news, the XO explained, the captain had retreated to his cabin and was rarely seen in the open, nonetheless the bridge. The XO brought reports, meals, and laundry into the captain's cabin, but the captain sat in the dark, wanting not to be bothered with the details of the final voyage. I asked if any of the dignitaries or I were going to interview the captain; the XO's expression turned comical. The captain, I learned, had ordered the executive officer to tell the admirals on board to "go fuck themselves" should they persist on seeing him. I thought I was going to meet a legend in the flesh, but it looked as if the legend had checked out and all that was left was a bitter carcass of a man.

Later that evening, the XO, the dignitaries, and I sat in the officer's mess and partook in the final meal the *Maelstrom* would have at sea. Besides the choppy water we were navigating through, with our dishes and drinks slightly sliding on the table, the meal was pleasant. One of the admirals wasn't as uptight as I'd thought, as he'd brought a handle of rum and ordered us each to take swigs. The senator, however, was a pompous prick and openly condemned the behavior before storming off to his cabin. The rum admiral, happily sloshed, gave the senator the finger and then told us how he'd earned his rank by starting out as a seaman and working his way up to admiral, unlike the senator who'd got his position through "kissing dick and sucking ass." We spent the night in the mess telling tales of war, lost loves, and drunken debacles, and we all drank to the final voyage of the USS *Maelstrom*.

The room was full with laughs, cigar smoke, and the smell of the sweet fermented sugar cane. I drank so much rum that I didn't notice the ship was rocking more harshly. I mentioned it to the rum admiral; he laughed and thought he'd gained his low tolerance back. Suddenly the ship violently pitched starboard, and I was thrown on top of the XO. He pushed me off and ran toward the bridge. The admirals and I ran behind, running on the bulkheads as we fought to keep our balance, the *Maelstrom* violently rocking back and forth. We made it to the bridge where the senator was already waiting for us, looking incredulous. The XO was about to demand a report, until he looked out the bridge and was left speechless.

I looked out into the ocean and felt the shivers of horror spread its icy touch through my entire body. The pale light of the crescent moon lit the storm growing before us. The horizon, to me, normally looked as if the sea falls of it in the end. Now, a black and gray wall surrounded us as massive blue bolts of lightning briefly lit the sky like the morning sun. The storm was massive and steadily growing around us, playing with its prey before it attacked. In the distance, waterspouts formed and dissipated, as they gathered strength. The wind howled a high-pitched wail, sharp enough to cause my ears to bleed. Faith in seeing the morning sun abandoned me as I came to terms that morning, for me, might not come. The *Maelstrom* rocked and pitched, and sailors on the bridge flew over their stations and into each other.

I looked to the XO for comfort. His expression was nothing but fear and misery. I scanned the faces of the others on the bridge and witnessed the twisted gnarl of despair displayed on their pale, flushed skin.

I wasn't a praying man, might have been an atheist if I put thought into it, but I prayed to any being listening. A lightning bolt that struck off the bow answered me, causing the lights to go out. In the pitch-blackness, the XO hollered for someone to get the engineer, but another bolt of lightning lit up the bridge. In the brief second of light, a stark silhouette darted past me and straight to a panel on the bulkhead. The bridge went black, until the lights returned and found me staring at the panel in awe.

When you hear of the stories of Captain Leroy Santos you might imagine a giant among men; he didn't disappoint in person. He was the tallest man on the bridge, and he had a powerful frame that shown through his impeccably worn dress blues. His hair was dark with graying temples; his skin was dark, but I could not tell if his color were natural or the result of years of sun at sea. It was his eyes, though, that made me fear him more than I feared the storm. Every step he took was deliberate. His shoulders rolled forward, his head slightly down, as if he were a boxer walking into the ring. The ship stopped pitching for the few moments it took for him to get to the wheel, as if his entrance were needed for everyone to see. The crew and dignitaries on the bridge forgot to fear the storm for those brief moments and watched in amazement as the legend took control of the *Maelstrom*.

The captain picked up the sound phone and barked orders in a deep and raspy voice. "Engine room! Give me every horsepower this old girl can give! We're going through this!" He slammed the phone back into its receiver and then addressed us. In all my life, I had never heard, nor would I ever hear a man take command as he had that night. "Men, this hurricane is growing on top of us, and it seems like its aim is for us not to see port again. The odds are against us as we cannot go back nor go around the storm, so I intend to go through this heartless bitch and get you guys home. Follow my command and you'll see dawn again." It was brief but effective and caused me to forget about death.

The senator, however, began to panic and told everyone that Captain Santos was insane. The senator demanded that one of the other admirals take command of the *Maelstrom*. They looked at each other, looked at Captain Santos, and then kept their positions. "He's going to get us all killed," the senator shrieked. "If you don't take command of the ship, then I will!" Fist raised, he ran toward Captain Santos. The senator went to throw a punch, but it never connected, as Captain Santos slammed his forehead into the nose of the senator and quickly went back to steering the ship. The senator lay unconscious on the deck, blood pouring from his collapsed nasal cavity.

We looked down at the senator, then at Captain Santos as he wiped the senator's blood from his forehead and stared straight ahead, sizing up the storm.

"Men, seal all hatches," the captain ordered. "Navigation, give me a bearing out of this storm. Radio, make contact with command and keep informing them of our position. The rest of you help the ship's crewmen, and somebody get that soft shit off my bridge. Move, move, move!" Everyone on the bridge ran in different directions, each admiral assisting in sealing the hatches or helping crewmen with their stations.

"I'm heading to the engine room. I know how to get this old girl fired up again," said the rum admiral as he went below.

I helped by dragging the senator out of sight of Captain Santos and used whatever first aid expertise I had to help stop the bleeding. Then, I strapped the senator and myself into the seats on the bridge and watched Captain Santos take the reins of the *Maelstrom* and steer her into the heart of the storm.

The old warship climbed and fell over the massive waves as we went deeper into the storm. The crew insanely took lines and tied themselves down to their posts, trusting their captain not to sink the ship, but Captain Santos was at ease at the helm. Fluid in his movements, matching the frequency of the old warship, he never flew off the deck.

Captain Santos picked up the sound phone and yelled, "Engine room, where is my power?"

I couldn't make out what was being said, but I could hear the voice of the rum admiral talking back to the captain. "You're afraid the engine might fail? How about you should be afraid of me, if you fail to get her moving again! What? No, you're wrong, motherfucker! She does have it! She hasn't failed us. She won't fail us! Now give me everything she's got!" Captain Santos ordered.

He slammed the phone down again and had his hand ready at the throttle. What I heard next was a song of beauty and wonder. The old ship's engines no longer cranked and coughed but sounded like a symphony of pure power. The *Maelstrom* was primed and ready for its last battle with its captain at the helm to live up to his legend.

The captain pushed the throttle forward and drove the ship into the heart of the watery hell. The crew felt the horror as we continued further into the nightmare; massive clouds, blacker than any void, swirled around us and glowed a devilish red after every lighting strike. Whirlpools formed across the bow of the ship. The wind and thunder roared continuously, like a ferocious beast of unimaginable size ready to gorge on the *Maelstrom* and her crew. Looking around, I saw the men turn white in terror.

Captain Santos unflinchingly stared down the storm and yelled out, "Not fucking tonight." He was no longer a mere man; he was a mythical hero charging into battle against the impossible.

The storm threw its worst at us, but the captain took it on. He sailed the ship in and out of the whirlpools, plunged into the waterspouts, and came out the other side and continued forward. Lightning bolts fell like mortar but missed as the captain dodged each bolt. This continued for an hour until the rain stopped and the waters calmed. We examined each other, hesitant to celebrate our survival, though we couldn't stop the sense of relief when minutes passed without being thrown around the bridge. I unbuckled myself, walked toward the nearest window, and watched the clouds slowly secede and the blue glow of the crescent moon break through the clouds. I smiled with joy at the stars and breathed easy again, until I looked at the horizon.

Something was approaching us in the distance, and it was coming fast.

The object confused me, as it increased in size while moving faster toward us. Captain Santos seemed to know, by instinct, what it was as he yelled for us to brace ourselves.

I, like a fool, continued to stare at the object until somebody screamed, "Tidal wave!" Shock overcame me as I starred in awe at the colossal size of the wave that charged forward. It reminded me of the first time I'd seen the Empire State Building as a child and of my fright at its enormity. I was staring at something that looked taller than the Empire State, wide as the horizon, and it charging straight at us.

I turned around expecting to see terror in the men's faces but, instead, witnessed the unexpected. The men did not show fear, not in their expression nor in their eyes; instead, they looked determined. They stared into the creature threatening to devour us in one gulp yet showed no terror, only the will to fight. It took me a second to understand why, until I saw the captain.

Captain Santos stared into the tidal wave, displaying only the audacity needed to inspire his men to fight a monster. His courage was infectious, as I was certain that no man felt fear on that bridge, only the willingness to fight for his life.

Looking upon Captain Santos no longer made me feel afraid of dying. I was angry. A savage rage seized my body as I turned around and starred down the tidal wave, prepared to fight the titan.

The wave approached faster and faster.

The captain pushed the throttle completely forward and charged to the tidal wave. "Men, I will not fail you! You will see the dawn again! As long as I am in command of this mighty ship, you will survive! YOU WILL LIVE!" he yelled as the ship began a violent vertical climb.

I marveled as the window broke. Water gushed out, causing me to fly to the back of the bridge, passing the men still tied to their stations. I landed against the bulkhead, hitting my head against a pipe. I tried to remain conscious, but the world grew black as the bridge flooded with water and the ship went vertical. The last images I saw were the captain standing fast against the rushing water, holding his position as the ship climbed up the tidal wave. I'm not sure if what I saw next was a hallucination, but I swore I saw a man dressed in a black suit standing next to Captain Santos saying, "Tell me your story."

I opened my eyes slowly. Everything was blurry, bright, and painful. I closed my eyes again and listened to the sounds of the gentle songs of seagulls and the welcoming sound of calm waves. I opened my eyes again and saw the glow of the morning sun engulfing the bridge and the rum admiral above me, smiling and gently wrapping a bandage around my head. We had survived. The legendary Captain Leroy Santos had kept his promise to his men and beat the odds.

Slowly, I sat up and looked around at the disheveled bridge and the senator sitting next to me, his face wrapped with white and bloodstained bandages. I stood and painfully walked to the weather deck to see the crew deploying the life rafts. The USS *Maelstrom* had fought her final battle and won gloriously. But, she took a savage beating and was now slowly sinking.

I walked back into the bridge. The captain stood proudly at the helm, steering the ship toward the horizon. I went to tell him that he should get to a raft, but the rum admiral stopped me and told me not to touch his body. Captain Leroy Santos had kept his promise to the men; the mad man fought against the odds and kept his men alive but at the cost of his life. He died at the helm of his beloved ship, never leaving his post.

I asked if we were going to take his body, but the rum admiral said to leave him, to let him be buried with his ship. It was an honor not many would understand.

I helped carry the wounded into the life rafts and then the useless senator. We were only floating for an hour when three rescue ships came and picked us up. We all stood on the weather decks of the rescue ships and watched the old warship slowly sink into the sea.

The XO pushed his way to the front of the men and stood at attention. "Present arms!" he yelled as he tried to hide the sad crackle in his voice.

Every sailor on the three rescue ships saluted the old warship and its captain. It took another forty-five minutes for the ship to sink, but all the sailors kept saluting until the USS *Maelstrom* and Captain Leroy Santos were laid to rest.

2 Miles

"Were you really frightened back there, or was that a trick to get me to show you that side of me and to transition into your next story?" Rick asked as he massaged his cramping hamstrings. The two were able to move quickly for the last mile, but the hike was starting to take a toll on his body. Rick's legs began to cramp. He could feel the blood and puss slowly ooze from the blisters on his feet. She was unfazed and seemed as if she wasn't even tired. She'd yet to break a sweat since starting the hike.

She used her hands to hike a steeper part of the trail. "A little bit of both. I'm afraid of the storm, but also I'm afraid you're too scared, maybe even stubborn, to tell me your story."

"If you know so much about me then why do you need to hear my story?"

"It's not so much me hearing your story but you hearing your own story out loud. You need to hear for yourself who you really are and what you did mattered."

Rick stopped for a moment as she went on ahead. She turned around as Rick looked at the ground. His massive frame was childlike as his posture changed into self-loathing. "What I did didn't matter. It didn't work. I'm not sure if I did it for the right reasons or if it helped anyone. Whenever I helped someone, it usually involved a debt, and I was the one who paid it. And sometimes that debt was too high, and I had enough paying for it after I lost everything in trying to help."

She placed her hand on his shoulder and made him look her in the eye. "Sometimes we make sacrifices to help others, to do good for the sake of good. At the moment we do it, we don't see the unintended consequences of our actions. We don't see the benefits of what we do, but you have to believe that what you did mattered and that you probably won't see the effects until years later. But good things happen when you put it all on the line. Good has a way of being viral."

The Runner

I want to stop and rest, but I can't. Many depend on me to complete this run. If I stop, then people will die. If I complete it, then lives will be saved. There will be peace if I deliver the message in my hand. My lungs burn with every breath I take, but I must not stop, for my family and all families depend on it.

I was told that I will have two sunrises to reach the battleground before both sides can attack. The truce in my hand passed directly to me from my king as he wisely heard reason for peace. Sneers and insults were thrown at me because he gave the task to a woman, but I pleaded my case in his court. Out of the men left in the kingdom, no one knew the trails of Greece better than I, and nobody can beat me on my stallion in any race.

They yelled blasphemy for me, a woman, trying to help stop a war, but I pleaded with all my heart to let me go because my son will die in battle if I do not stop it. My husband, my love of my life, died in the last war; what if I could save my son and the love of others from dying?

They rationalized with the king the treacherousness of my path, the dangers from the mighty mountains, the savages and the wild beasts, but I pleaded to my king that I cannot fail, because I must not fail. My king, my wise king, handed me the treaty with his seal and ordered me to deliver peace.

I rode off on my noble steed within that hour, only taking a spear and sword, as I raced into the mountains against the falling sun.

That was one sundown ago. My horse broke its legs in a trap set by hunters. I mercifully killed my mighty horse to set him free from his pain. But his sacrifice was not in vain; he got me over the mountain. Since then I have been running.

Through the forest I ran, its sharp brush and jagged cliffs slicing open my skin, but I run on because I have to. I push on even though I feel the blood slowly pour from my feet and out my leather sandals. My joints burn, crackle, and pop with ever step I take. I want to scream in agony, for the excruciating cramping of my muscles. I want to stop. I want to rest and let my body heal, but I can't, for my brave son.

I climb a hill and that is where I see the glorious sight — two armies in the far distance. I take a painful breath of relief as I watch them still in their camps for the night. I want to celebrate, but I cannot because the sun is going to rise and the battle will commence.

I start my run down the hill, but my sandal loses its grip and slips on a jagged rock. I tumble down the hill. Falling and falling, for what feels ages, until I land hard on the jagged bottom. I lay there for a moment and breath. I don't feel it at first but the pain intensifies.

I slowly feel my way to my stomach, where the rough edge of the sharp stone dagger pierces bellow my stomach. I want to lie down and cry but I can't. My son needs me. I reach down and dislodge the phallic stone from myself. A flow of warm blood pulsates out. I grab a handful of earth and plug the gaping hole, then tear a piece of cloth from my sash and bind my wound. I carefully roll over and push myself off the ground, but the pain is overwhelming and I fall back down.

I cry in agony for a moment until I hear the cries of my brave son when he was an infant. Those cries he wailed when he fell running for the first time. Those cries I could not deny; he still cries for me, and I cannot fail him. I pick myself up and cry in pain, but I start running again.

I have been running for hours, and I want to give in to my exhaustion and let go of the excruciating pain across my body. I want to die. I slow down and fall to the ground; my eyes begin to close as I feel the comforting embrace of death. I see the first rays of the morning sun break free above the camping armies.

"This is it, I am done," I say.

I am about to accept failure and welcome the rest much needed until I see an image of my brave son. I see him as a child playing with his friends, as a young man lovingly kissing his wife, and as a dead soldier lying mutilated on the battleground with other sons of mothers.

"No," I scream out into the wild. "No! I must not give in! There will be peace! There shall be peace for my son!"

The pain subsides as I feel rejuvenated with the thought of my son dying. I take a deep breath and painfully push myself off the ground. I take one step forward and scream in pain. I take another and another and another until I am running again. I run faster and harder than I have ever run in my life.

The cracking of sinew and bone grows intense as I keep running to the battlefront. I am so close, and to stop now would mean war. The pain becomes unbearable, and I vomit on myself as I kept running, but I don't slow down.

I take deep breaths, but each one makes my lungs burn. I try to focus on the end, how close it is, but I vomit again and wipe my mouth with my hand, only to see a wet chunky crimson gleam underneath the moonlight, but I do not stop. Tears stream from my eyes, and I beg for it to be over. I pray to the gods for them to end my pain, but I think of my son and I run faster.

The sun rises as I make it to the edge of the battlefield where the two great armies march toward each other, flying their colors, chanting their prayers, and grabbing their spears tightly for their war. The explosive sounds of the war drums pound their frightening melody, causing my body to shake as I make my approach between the two converging armies.

I run between the two armies and scream, "STOP!" as I finally halt to breathe. The morning sun warms my face, and I look down at my bloody body and the treaty in my hand. I lift the treaty above my head and then fall to my knees out of exhaustion.

"Mother?" I hear a familiar voice scream.

My eyes blur, but I can see a soldier break ranks and run toward me.

He drops his shield and spear as he gets closer and catches me as I collapse to the ground. My brave son holds me in his arms. I look upon his lovely smile, which warms my weakening heart. His warm tears fall upon my cheek and wash the blood and dirt from my face. I put my hand on his armor to feel his heart one more time.

"Somebody help me!" he screams to whomever would come. I hear the running of feet and clanking of armor from the opposite direction, and I see him unsheathe his sword and aim in that direction.

"No," says the enemy soldier. "Here is our healer. Please, let us help her."

My son stares at them uneasy, but he lets down his sword and lets the healer examine my broken body. I hold the treaty tightly in my hand until I see the two opposing generals meet in front of me. The sun grows brighter for them, but my world grows darker for me. With the last of my strength, I lift the treaty and its seal to both generals. One takes it and reads out loud for all to hear. At the end of the reading, both generals look each other in the eye and shake hands. The order is given and both sides stand down; there will be no war.

I can no longer see the sun, but I can still see my brave son's beautiful face as bright as day. He is crying uncontrollably as I take my final breaths. I put my hand on his face for the last time and say, "For you, my son, there will be peace. There will be peace. . . ."

The Hero of Harper High School: A Ballad for Jordan Ford

It has been ten years since I graduated from Harper High School in Chicago. It's a miracle I was never arrested for the things I did when I was younger, and it's even more of a miracle I didn't cross that line ten years ago. As I sit here recalling the events that took place when I was seventeen, I'm still left in wonder and awe over the case of Jordan Ford.

Ten years ago was the fall of 2015, and I was a senior in high school. I was a decent student, making above average grades. My teachers thought of me as smarter than I believed myself to be, but I never saw it at the time. I played varsity football as a running back and was close to setting records for the district. This would seem like a normal childhood until you realized where I lived in Chicago. I lived in what we called, and slowly the world would know as, "Chi-raq," one of the most violent places to live in America.

The media liked to focus on the War on Terrorism, the Kardasians, or cop-killing blacks; but you never heard about the black-on-black killings taking place in my old neighborhood. The constant shootings on the corners made it seem normal, as if you lived in the suburbs and the ice cream man had come by. In defense of the police, they did try to solve the murders, but nobody would snitch, out of some false sense of mistrust or the real fear of gang retaliation.

The gangs in our neighborhood were numerous, starting from the Bloods and the Cripps to the many other gangs that broke off from these two factions. It's sad to think back on this, but back then, we were forced to pick a gang for protection due to the intense rivalry between all the gangs, and if you were "solo" then you were likely to be a victim to a brutal beating or things worse that only a deprived adolescent could conjure up.

I joined the Chi-raiders, a wannabe gang that only peddled dope for some low level drug dealers. I chose them because they rarely got involved in anything violent, and they let me be for most of the time. Once and a while I had to be their muscle in some deals, had to bruise a couple of other gangbanger's ribs, but I didn't do anything that bad. It was like something out of the Middle East's tribal wars and honor killings in Harper High. We had guys on the football team who were great friends suddenly beating each other to a bloody pulp because their respective gangs went to battle.

Then there were the stabbings in school and the shootings outside of it, all meant to send a message to the other gang in charge. I stopped making friends after my sophomore year because two of them ended up dead and the third tried stabbing me with a pencil because his gang had demanded it for his initiation. How could there be places like this in America? It was even worse for the solos, who were often the target of initiation beatings or used for target practice. Toward the end of my senior year, most students were in a gang, but Jordan Ford changed everything.

He was an odd guy. First, he was blacker than me, which is hard because my complexion is similar to coal. Extremely thin almost to the point of malnourishment, his hair was nappy and unkempt, lint always sticking out of it. He wore the same three set of clothes every week and kept to himself. He had no friends and rarely spoke to anyone, but he was smart, extremely smart. He was on track to becoming valedictorian. The oddest thing about Jordan was that he never looked people in the eye. He mostly looked down when talking to someone or stared past a person, but he never looked anyone in the eye.

Jordan was a solo, but for the longest time nobody had picked on him. He walked home alone every day, but the gangs never bothered him because they didn't think much of him and considered him some mental defect. All this changed my senior year.

At the time, Harper Hill teachers and coaches were doing the best they could to get graduating students out of the "war zone" by setting them up with college and military recruiters, helping them with college applications, and applying for scholarships. My coach was trying to get me into college on a football scholarship, but I didn't think I was good enough for college. I felt like I was going to be judged as some nigger or a thug and my 'hood was the place I belonged.

Around this time violence increased in the school. Too many gangs were vying for power and flexing their muscles by the battles in and out of school. That year Harper High earned the record for most students shot in US history. Every day for two months at least one, if not two, students went to the hospital for gang-related reasons. Some of those victims were set on fire because the gangs wanted to remind us that hell was on earth.

Everyone had at that point joined a gang for protection expect for one: Jordan Ford. He was the only solo left, and the rumors were going around about making him into an example for his defiance. The teachers got hold of it and offered him a ride home or a police escort, but he outright refused and still walked alone, despite the danger to his life. Then one day we saw him walk into class with a busted lip and a swollen eye. He didn't say anything, but we all heard that one gang took him into the alley and gave him a beating so they could claim credit for breaking the defiant Jordan Ford.

I didn't put much thought into it until the end of the school day, when I met up with the Chi-raiders and watched Jordan Ford walk home.

We watched as he walked alone, not looking worried nor terrified but indifferent. We watched him make it to the next block, where he was corned by the Bloods, who without notice pummeled him right there on the sidewalk, where the neighborhood and students could witness. They kicked and punched him severely, to the point that I had to walk away because I couldn't look anymore. The last image I remember was a mist of blood coming from his mouth when one of the Bloods kicked him in the stomach.

I prayed he would not come to school the next day. I prayed he would learn a lesson and stop defying the warped culture set in place . . . but he didn't. The next day he came to class limping, barely able to move his left arm, but he sat in his desk and kept to himself. The teachers brought him to the principal office and begged him not to walk alone anymore. He answered them by walking out the office.

At the end of the day, a large group of students watched from across the street as Jordan Ford walked out of the school doors and down the street by himself. I couldn't help but think how much of an idiot this guy was at the time, but now that I am older, I understand why. He again walked alone and was this time met by the Cripps, who wasted no time in savagely beating him. We all watched Jordan be pummeled again, a small pool of blood growing on the cement. He laid lifeless on the corner as they jumped in their Crown Vic and peeled down the street. We all stood there, disillusioned at witnessing another murder, until we saw him move. He slowly and painfully picked himself up and began limping home.

He kept doing this for two weeks, a different gang gave him a beating every day. I cringed in pity every time I saw him in the morning with his fresh injuries, but miraculously he was still walking. It was almost mystical how he took those beatings and kept coming the next day. There was no way a normal person could survive that type of bodily punishment, and the truly admirable thing was that he never begged or cried; he endured. He unknowingly made a legend of himself as "the nigger who defied the gangs." Students were slowly starting to rebel and started to disavow their affiliation and walk home by themselves. The gang leaders saw Jordan Ford no longer as some "retarded nigger" but as a threat to their power. "How dare this punk ass nigger defy the order of things," they would say.

Then, fate stepped in on a beautiful spring afternoon. I was about to head home until my gang grabbed me and brought me into a dark alley near the school. T-Mob, our leader, took out a nickel-platted Colt and placed it in my hand. I was confused because I'd never had to use a gun on any of my deals, but then he gave me his order: kill Jordan Ford.

Jordan Ford had became a threat to the gangs. Students were quitting and no longer paying their dues, and then the rumors were spreading that the other gangs were planning to gun him down to send a message. T-Mob wanted it to be the Chi-raiders to kill Jordan Ford so they could have the bragging rights and move up in power. T-Mob wanted me to pull the trigger. I went to hand the gun back, but he took out his black Glock from his waistband and aimed it at me.

"If you don't shoot that nigger, then I'm gonna cap your ass with this," T-Mob threatened.

I nervously tucked the Colt into my waistband and walked in front of T-Mob and the other members as we moved to hide in the alley on Jordan Ford's route.

I prayed to God that Jordan Ford decided to take the police on their offer for a ride or that he'd walked a different route, but whoever was listening had different plans as T-Mob walked out of the alley and disappeared out of sight. A few moments later, I saw a pitiful body fall to the ground before me. Jordan Ford slowly picked himself up and tried to walk out, but T-Mob kicked him in the knees and Jordan collapsed on the ground. I stood there mortified, hoping this would be some scare tactic, but all I heard was T-Mob screaming at me to shoot.

I looked down at Jordan, his head down, struggling to stand back up. I kept shaking my head as T-Mob circled behind me. Next thing I felt was the barrel of his Glock on the back of my skull as he screamed at me to shoot Jordan Ford. To this day, I cannot recall taking out the Colt. I just remember it already being in my hands, aimed at Jordan's head. I pressed the barrel into his forehead so I could steady my violently shaking hands. I heaved as my stomach painfully cramped, wanting to vomit out my lunch. Tears ran down my eyes as I begged T-Mob to let Jordan be, to not make me kill him. The other Chi-raiders looked nervously at each other like they disagreed with T-Mob, but they were too cowardly to say something.

"Bitch, yo' ass better cap this cunt in the next ten seconds," T-Mob screamed. "Ten . . . nine . . ." he counted as he pressed the Glock harder against my head.

I started to squeeze the trigger, but then Jordan lifted his gaze and looked straight into me. There was no fear. There were no tears. Only his eyes locked onto my eyes and all I saw was courage and pity. He was brave and defiant, even in the face of death.

"Five . . .four . . ." T-Mob kept counting down to remind me of my pending death. I kept staring in awe into Jordan's gaze, wondering how he could be so brave.

"Three . . . two . . ." I heard T-Mob's finger pull back the trigger.

"One . . ." I suddenly pulled my head to the right and spun my right elbow across my back and hit the Glock out of T-Mob's hands.

The Glock flew into the corner of the alley and T-Mob lost his balance. Then I slammed the handle of the Colt furiously into T-Mob's face as he fell to the ground. Blood gushed out his mouth and nose as I busted open his face.

He sucker punched me and I lost my footing over him. T-Mob started to crawl to the Glock and was about to pick it up until I stomped my foot on his hand and heard the soft snaps of bone break in his fingers and wrist. He screamed in agony as I snatched up the Glock and aimed both guns at his forehead. I was about to pull the triggers until I saw Jordan struggle to stand. Despite the violence done to him, he never gave in. He became the best of us, not the monster like the man I was about to shoot or the man I was about to become.

I kicked T-Mob in the face and knocked him out cold. I looked around to the other members and told them I was done; I was no longer part of their gang. They looked at each other and slowly walked out the alley, leaving the gang as well. I started to strip the guns apart, something I'd learned off the movies and YouTube, and dumped them into the sewer grates. But, when I got to T-Mob's Glock, I found that the coward hadn't even loaded it with bullets.

Jordan Ford stood, straightened himself out, and picked up his backpack. He took out the bloodstained towel from his backpack and wiped his mouth, then quietly walked out of the alley. I went to follow him but he stopped.

Without looking my way, he said, "I walk alone." He limped back into the daylight and headed homeward.

I left T-Mob in the alley and walked back to school to ask my coach if he could help with my college applications.

A week later the school was turning a new leaf. Shootings dropped, students were slowly getting out of the gangs, and I was applying for college. Jordan Ford still walked home alone but with no one beating him anymore. Things were looking optimistic, until Friday. It was the start of spring break and a large group of the students walked together to the block party a few blocks away from the school. I saw Jordan walk alone to his house, and I jogged over to him to invite him to come with us, then I saw T-Mob dash around the corner and aim his gun into Jordan's head. Time froze as I watched in horror and witnessed the look of hate on T-Mob's disfigured face and the look of courage on Jordan's.

"Beg for your life, nigga! Come on, beg!" T-Mob screamed.

Jordan looked unflinchingly into T-Mob's eyes and answered with unwavering courage, "No."

I don't remember hearing or seeing the gun fire; I just saw Jordan's bloodied body lying on the ground, T-Mob yelling over him, "Don't fuck with T-Mob." Then he ran off. I stood in shock in the middle of the street, paralyzed until the police came and pulled me off the road. A large group of people circled around the cops as they began stringing up the yellow tape and draping the white cloth over Jordan's body.

I never saw the neighborhood cry in unison over one dead kid before. Detectives came and were reluctant to ask for witnesses since history told them that nobody rats. They were surprised, though, as multiple witnesses stepped forward and testified to the murder, even giving the name and address of T-Mob.

A few hours later, police raiding his house, T-Mob tried to blow his brains out. Too bad for him that he didn't aim the gun high enough and blew part of his jaw off instead. He was sentenced to death a year later. I testified against him at trial.

It's been ten years since the death of Jordan Ford, but he did something that the police, politicians, and the NAACP couldn't do. He brought change to my neighborhood. Gang violence plummeted, shootings dropped to a record low, and Harper High became one of the best schools for inner-city kids. I'm not sure if Jordan Ford planned to take a stand, or if he did what he did because he didn't know better, but he made a miracle happen. He became known as the Hero of Harper High and a saint to the neighborhood. As for me, ten years later, I no longer think people see me as a nigger or a thug; they just see me as a doctor of oncology at the Mayo Clinic.

1 Mile

"We have one mile to go, and I feel like I should have kept the gun because dying of dehydration is not the way I wanted to go," Rick said as he painfully limped forward.

She ignored his morbid comment as she gracefully climbed over a tall ledge on the trail. Rick followed her lead but lost his grip on the ledge and fell backwards, his right ankle catching on the stone he'd used to step off. A snap was heard and Rick moaned in pain. She jumped from the ledge and went to his aid as Rick tried to stand back up, but he screamed when he put weight on his foot. She helped him sit down on a boulder and tenderly unfastened the strings to his boot and slid it off. Rick's foot was blackened and bruised around the ankle.

"You either sprained it or broke it," she said, grabbing two sturdy branches lying nearby. Without asking, she reached for Rick's waist and began unfastening his belt. Rick's look of agony changed into a bashful smile.

"Are you about to make me feel better?" he asked.

She blushed at Rick's advances.

"No, I need to make a splint so that we can keep you moving." She then took the belt off Rick's waist and tightly wrapped it around his ankle and the two branches. She then grabbed a longer branch and gave it to Rick. "Here, use it as a crutch."

Rick gingerly stood back up and took a step forward. Still in pain, but not as painful as before, he attempted to climb over the ledge again.

"Why do you keep going, Rick?" she asked. "Why didn't you just lie there and quit? Why didn't you just chamber another round in your pistol and pull the trigger again?"

Rick stood there dumbfounded as he started to realize why she was asking those questions. Why did he keep going? Why didn't he just finish the job and use one of the other ten bullets?

Rick kept trying to think of an excuse, but she cut him off as he tried to utter it. "Don't answer, because I don't want to hear the excuses anymore," she said sternly. "You threw the gun away and decided to follow me because you don't want to give in. I know you too well. You're a fighter, and you would rather go out fighting than give in. And you're a rebel too. You would rather be the outcast, take a path alone when you're asked to conform to something you know is wrong. You don't want to die; you're at a tipping point."

Rick stopped at the bend of the road, at the sign for the half-mile mark, the steepest part of the trail. He sat down on the trail and looked to the east, the storm growing more savage and approaching steadily. Rick shivered as the temperature started to drop, the wind growing stronger.

"Who are you?"

"I have one more story to tell you, and it explains who I am and what you really are."

Tell Me Your Story

On a frigid, snowy February evening in Chicago sat a pub several blocks east of Wrigley Field, not a tourist spot but a neighborhood pub beloved by the locals, a warm and inviting place where framed pictures of the locals hung on the walls. The pub had been closed for a week because of the blizzard that consumed the Second City, but tonight the pub reopened, and to no surprise to the bartender, the place was dead. Besides two local drunks, the pub was just her and her misery.

The bartender didn't mind the slow business and expected to close early; tomorrow was the second anniversary of her fiancé's death. The bartender was known to be chipper and warm to her patrons, but they all knew not to bother her on the night before and on the anniversary of his death. She liked to go to work on those two nights because it helped her to stop thinking of her beloved.

The man who killed her fiancé was an exhausted local plumber who drove over black ice and lost control of his work truck just as her fiancé was crossing the road. The police investigation found the man not guilty of any crime, and he wasn't arrested. The fiancé's family, a compassionate people, forgave the man for killing their son, but the bartender could not, for he was the love of her life. If there were every such a thing as soul mates and true love, then she had it with her fiancé. He was perfect to her, and they both adored each other so much that every day they had together was like dating for the first time. He had shown her so much beauty in her life, but now on this night, she was reminded that people, romantic notions, and happiness die. Every day for a year she begged for death to take her. A life without him was not a life worth living, and tonight she contemplated killing herself. Part of her wanted to live, but the other part of her wanted to die so that she could find relief from her broken heart.

Home by Edward Sharpe and the Magnetic Zeros began to play over the pub speakers.

The bartender ran to the stereo system and turned it off. Before last year, she would sing for the patrons on the weekends, for her voice was as lovely as the sound of summer rain falling on a roof. People would fill the pub and gleefully listen to her voice as she sang just for the joy of singing, but *Home* was the song she only sang for her fiancé when he visited her at work. The song had played when they met. He had played it during his proposal to her. Since his death, she had stopped singing and cringed in pain whenever she heard it play.

The night was growing older, and she busied herself with cleaning behind the bar until she saw the two local drunks sloppily don their heavy coats and stumble into the frigid night. The bartender sighed as she was now alone in the bar. Twenty minutes went by and nobody else walked into the pub. The bartender looked at her watch. It was five minutes to midnight. She decided to close the pub early. She walked into the back to retrieve the envelopes for the bank deposit and was startled to find a man sitting at the end of the bar. The bartender did not hear the door open, and she was only gone for less than ten seconds.

She regained her composure and quickly accessed the mysterious man sitting at her bar. The man was wearing an immaculate black suit with a black silk tie and a white French cuff dress shirt. He looked to be in his late twenties, but something in his dark brown eyes made him seem older. The bartender was mesmerized for a few moments as she tried to figure out why he looked both young and old at the same time, but then he smiled and it snapped her back into the moment. It was a bright reassuring smile that made her feel comfortable. She felt he meant no harm.

Walking to him, she asked politely, "What can I get for you?"

The man eased forward on his bar stool and scanned over the selection of spirits on the wall. "I'll have an Old Fashioned. Make it neat," he said, still giving her that reassuring smile.

The bartender began muddling the orange and cherry into the rock glass, then asked, "Did you just come from a date?"

The man, seemingly confused by the question, took a moment to realize why she'd asked and then answered, "Oh, because of the suit. No, I just came off work."

The bartender thought this was odd because it was close to midnight, and she didn't see an overcoat on any of the coat racks. "So what is it you do?" She served him the Old Fashioned.

The man sipped the cocktail. He appeared to savor the drink before swallowing. "I'm a judge," he answered modestly.

"Really? Judge who, and of what?" she asked, wondering his name.

"Judge Jaydee, but I'm not the type of judge you're thinking of," he said, as he picked up the glass and took another swig.

Confused by the answer, the bartender was hoping "judge" wasn't code for a hitman or if *Jaydee* was just the name for a yuppie high of some glamour drug. "What type of judge are you?" she asked.

He reached for the bowl of pretzels and remarked, "I'm a judge of man."

"Like you judge men for competitions?"

Jaydee smiled and sighed. "In order to explain what I do, I would have to tell you a story, but I have two terms before I tell you this story."

The bartender felt sudden unease. The man didn't look threatening, if anything he was putting her at ease, but there was something off about him. Curiosity was getting the best of her. "Name the terms," she said.

"The first is to be open minded regarding the story I'm about to tell. It will be unbelievable, but I assure you it's true. You'll think I am mad and a liar, but you'll be right on one of those accounts. I ask you please to listen until the end; this story has a message. Do you agree with the first term?"

She nodded, "What's the second one?"

"Please make me another Old Fashioned, sweetie," he said as he gulped the one in his hand.

The bartender made him another and handed it to him. As she pulled her hand away, he gently grabbed it and looked her in the eyes, saying, "Please listen until the very end." His face, being of a young man's features but with the eyes of an old man, seemed sincere and no threat to her. "I will," she said, "just tell your story."

He sipped his Old Fashioned and asked, "Do you believe in angels and demons?"

"Not anymore."

"For most, people believe that there are angels and demons, but they do not know about the other beings. Sometime after the beginning of man's era on earth, the devil and God met to talk about the souls of man. The devil argued with God about who should be the one to determine if man should go to paradise or into the inferno. Since both sides did not trust each other, they came to an accord; the fate of humanity would be placed in man's hands, so the judges were created. Judges would be formerly deceased men and women who had shown to be impartial in difficult decisions and who were known to have an innate ability in judging a person's character."

A cold chill crawled down the bartender's spine as she realized she was now alone with a madman. She considered hitting the panic alarm underneath the bar counter but something told her to keep listening.

"God believed man would be of better fit to weigh the souls of humanity because man knew the struggles humanity had to go through in life. While the devil believed the accord would get more souls on his side because mankind would let bias, hatred, and irrational thinking get the better of itself." Jaydee stopped swig from his Old Fashioned and signaled for the bartender to make another. "Now the judges aren't Death. They're a different department. You can think of us as processors and Death, or reapers as we call them, as logistics. We meet with someone who's about to die within twelve hours of his or her death — "

"Why twelve hours?" the bartender interrupted as she made another Old Fashioned.

"The future is unpredictable up to a certain point with us, too many variables, especially with humans. The judges get their assignments within twelve hours, and we meet with the person anytime within that timeframe. Sometimes we have time to meet with the person in a private location, say the person's bedroom, where we talk and have him or her forget before letting the person go out on his or her last day. Other times, we meet with the person within the last moments of life, in which we slow down time and begin listening to the person's story."

She took a deep breath and argued with herself if it was wise to feed into the man's morbid delusions, but her curiosity won out. "Why make them forget? They're about to die that day, so why make them forget? And how can you stop time?"

"It's the whole predicting the future thing. We work on the same relative dimension as you, and we know how to take liberty with physics, but predicting the future is difficult because of the Heisenberg's uncertainty principle, so—"

"Heisenberg's what?"

"Google it later. Just know the variables become drastically reduced within the twelve-hour time frame where we can predict a person's death. The variables take in account for the person's health, age, job, time of day leaving work, yada yada yada. That technical stuff usually hurts my head. I leave that science to the section of the judges who hand out the assignments. We make them forget because we can't let them change their minds about the decisions they will have to make on their last day. You might be thinking it would be nice to give 'em a heads up on their last day, but there are grave consequences."

"Such as?"

"A person . . . or people might take their places," he said dryly. "When your time is up, then it's your time to leave."

The bartender began to relax a little and decided to play along with Jaydee's delusions. It was the most creative and intriguing story she'd heard in a long time. "So, do you guys have offices?"

"Believe it or not, we do, in every major city and township across the planet. We even have an office in Antarctica too."

"Since you are 'judges,' I take it you have formerly living judges and attorneys as colleagues?" the bartender asked.

"Ironically, no. I mean we do have some former judges and lawyers, but they're a minority within the department. I did meet two former US Supreme Court justices happily working in the afterlife. We have doctors and nurses, a few politicians, garbage men, farmers, but a good bulk of us come from first responders and former military. We have former generals and privates, medics and corpsman, EMTs and freighters, and police."

"Why so many of you guys?"

"It's because we chose professions in which we had to make the difficult decisions to help save lives. The reapers on the other hand are not grim or macabre as stories lead them to be. They are extremely warm and sympathetic people. No matter what verdict we hand out about the souls, they always calm the person as they take their last breaths and gently guide them to the next life. The reapers come from medical careers, such as nurses and doctors, and former members of religious order, nuns, monks, and priest.

"So what did you do before you died?"

Jaydee's face became solemn as he put his drink back on the bar top and looked down in silence for a moment. "I was a cop," he said, studying his drink.

The bartender hesitated briefly, then asked, "How did you die?"

Jaydee lifted his head, gazed into the bartender's eyes, and gave her a reassuring smile again. She saw a hidden sadness in his eyes.

"Back in the winter of 1966, I had just become a detective for the Chicago Police Department. It was a wonderful moment in my life because becoming a detective had always been a dream of mine, but sadly, my dream only lasted for a day. On my first official day of work, I stopped at a grocery store to pick up a pack of smokes. I remember walking in the back of the grocery store to check myself out in the mirror, as I was wearing a new suit for my first day on the job. As I walked back up front, I saw a young man sweating and nervously shaking in front of the checkout. Before I could put two and two together, the young man brandished a pistol and pointed it at the cashier. The young man stuttered, demanding the cashier hand over the money. At the time I thought the young man had tunnel vision; he never looked in my direction, so I decided to take him by surprise and reached for my .38 special."

Jaydee gulped his drink and paused for a few moments to regain his composure before starting again. "As I raised my gun, he quickly looked in my direction, and the next thing I know, I saw multiple flashes of light. Oddly, I didn't hear gunshots, just the loud pounding of my heart. My eyes adjusted from the flashes of light, and I realized I was staring at the tiles of the grocery store ceiling. I tried to move but had no control of my limbs. I panicked, coughing and heaving, and my lungs filled up with blood. I tried to scream for help but nobody came. Then, everything faded to black.

"As I took my final breath, I regretted only one thing in my life. I'd never fallen in love and had a family. That was the next thing I was going to set out to accomplish, but at that moment, I regretted not knowing what it was like to love and to be loved. As I thought this, I became furious and wanted to go kill the man who'd just taken my life. I felt myself taking the last gulp of air and crying, as I could no longer fight my way to life. As I closed my eyes I heard a gentle voice ask, 'Jaydee, do you want a job?' The next thing I knew I was sitting on a park bench in Hyde Park with a thick-bearded man who introduced himself as Edward Teach."

"Wait, Blackbeard was your mentor?" said the flabbergasted bartender.

"Yeah," chuckled Jaydee, "he became a judge by accident. "There was a mistake in his paperwork when he died; he was given a job instead of being judged. It took a decade for upper management to realize the mistake, but he became one of the best judges we have, so they decided to keep him working as to atone for his infamous life.

"Teach, he likes to be called that, had me shadow him for three years so that I could learn how to weigh a man's soul. During this training, I was taught about what we must ask for before deciding their fate."

"Which are?"

"First, I ask them to tell me their story."

"Their story?"

Jaydee stared starkly at the bartender. "Yes, their story. Please don't interrupt, because we're getting to the important part."

The bartender sheepishly looked away in embarrassment, but Jaydee gave her a warm forgiving smirk.

"Everyone has a story to tell, and everyone deserves to have their story heard, so before we weigh their souls, we ask them to tell us their stories, after which we ask them the two most important questions in their last moments of life: What is the best thing they have done? What is the worst thing they have done?

"For the first few years, I was a miserable ass. I mean, I did my job right, but all I thought about was the man who killed me. He took my life for a handful of fucking cash! He took away my goals, my future, my dream of finding a good woman and loving her until I was old and withered. The selfish bastard took my life because he didn't have the decency to do the hard and honest thing by getting a freaking job and doing right by society. . . ." Pausing for a few moments, Jaydee turned his head and stared out the window at the light flurries of snow falling outside. "All I wanted was to fall in love."

"I was angry and full of regret, but I slowly began enjoying the job and appreciating the importance of it. I heard people's stories; some were short and tragic while others were long and boring because of their fear to live. Then others . . . others were fantastic!" Jaydee's face lit up with a feverish excitement. "Full of fire, love, and passion. Stories of love, loss, and love again; stories about enduring insurmountable odds and coming out on top. These stories were better than any book or movie because they were real, and I was fortunate to hear them.

"But then there were the dark stories. I've heard horrifying stories of the cruelty of which man is capable. You think demons are evil? Man can be worse."

A chill went down the bartender's spine. "Man can be cruel but life can be crueler," she said, wiping the tear from her eye as she thought of her fiancé.

"Yes, but it can be so rewarding too. A year ago, I was assigned back to Chicago for a few months. At the time, I hadn't been in Chicago since I was killed, so you can only imagine the depression I felt as I walked around my native city. For the past fifty years, I've made an effort of moving on by traveling the world and focusing on my job I've come to love. Then on an evening, much like tonight, I was given an assignment to visit an old man who was breathing his final breaths. I walked into his house unnoticed as a large congregation of the man's family consoled each other in the living room. His family was quite large, which extended from his children to his great grandchildren. I walked through the hallways filled with photos of the man and his family on vacations, working on cars, and at holidays. It seemed like the man had a full life and it was his time to go. I walked into his bedroom and saw the old man's wife crying as she held onto his hand while her daughter and son tried to comfort her, but they could barely hold back their tears.

"I stopped time and made my approach to the graying man. He looked up and made a facial expression of recognition before saying, 'I knew you would be the face that would come get my soul.' I didn't understand why he said that but the man looked familiar to me also; maybe he was a man I'd arrested a lifetime ago. I then proceeded with the assignment.

"'Please, tell me your story,' I said. The old man started to tell me how the beginning of his life was filled with tragedy; his mother had died in front of him in a car accident when he was seven, and his father drank himself to death when he was ten. The old man bounced around foster homes until he turned eighteen and began living on the street. He took a job as a mechanic but was soon fired because of his growing addiction to crack cocaine, which had made its way to the streets for the first time. The old man then started stealing copper pipes and burglarizing people's homes to help feed his addiction. I listened carefully and began feeling a growing admiration for the old man. It was obvious that he'd turned his life around from his sad origins. But the admiration quickly disappeared when he said, 'I've never hurt anyone until the day I met you.' I was confused, but deep down I knew why he looked familiar, though I couldn't bring myself to acknowledge that gut feeling.

"I stared into the man's eyes and then came to terms with who he was. 'That morning was the lowest I've gotten in my life. I was desperate for a high, and I wanted that high badly. The night before I'd broken into a house and stolen a gun from inside. I was going to hawk it, but that morning I decided to try robbing a bodega to make some quick cash. I'd never held a gun before, and I remember my hand shaking uncontrollably as I hid it in my pocket when I entered. I don't remember anything before I fired the gun, but I've a vivid memory of you lying on the ground bleeding all over the floor,' said the old man.

"I felt the rage build inside as I stared into the eyes of my murderer. A thousand feelings and thoughts flooded me at once. He ended up with the family I'd wanted and never paid for what he'd done. I was about to scream, 'Go to hell,' which would have literally happened if I'd said it, but I restrained myself and reluctantly asked him to continue with his undeserving life story.

'I went to help you,' he explained, 'but ran out of the store when I saw your badge surrounded by an ocean of blood. I didn't even remember thinking about running away. I just saw the badge and ran as fast as I could. I ran and ran until I collapsed in a desolate alley. I had prayed it was a dream when I awoke, but I looked down at my pants and hands with your blood on them. I vomited in that alley and wailed because I'd killed a good man. I looked around for the gun I'd shot you with, but somebody must have taken it when I passed out. I still had the cash from the robbery and decided to kill myself in a poetic justice way by overdosing. I went to the nearest dealer and bought as much as I could with the cash. I injected the large dosage and felt the last moments of bliss before my one-way trip to hell.'

"'I don't know why I was spared,' he went on, 'but when I came too in the hospital, I looked up and saw an angel helping me. She's been with me ever since.' Then, the old man looked over to his wife. 'She took pity on me and nursed me back to health. I thought about committing suicide every morning, but she made me change my mind every day. She got me clean and had me working again, but every day you were on my mind.

Every day I lived wasn't deserved. You were my secret burden. The days turned into years as we started a family and my love for her grew, but I've never told her or anyone else of that fateful day. I could never atone for your death, and I knew hell was always going to be my final destination, but I was given a piece of heaven with her and my family before I would get what I deserved.'

"I sat there listening to the old man's story and started to feel conflicted. I didn't know what to do. I didn't know how to react. All I thought about after my death was sending him to hell. To my disgust, I was starting to feel sorry for him. I asked him the questions, 'What is the best thing you have done?' He looked to his wife and said, 'Loving her.' I then asked him, 'What is the worst thing you have done?' The old man began to cry as he looked me in the eye and said, 'That I let a good man pay the price for my life.' He then reached over and opened the drawer to his nightstand, took out an envelope, and placed it on the stand. I walked over to the stand, opened the envelope, and read his confession. 'I raised a good family. They will honor you by releasing my confession to the authorities. If you're ready, then take me to my deserved fate.'

The bartender was enthralled by his tale and eagerly asked, "Did you send him to hell?"

"I read and re-read his confession and then looked at his wife, his kids, and the pictures of them on the wall. The photos of his children were of them graduating from college, wearing white lab coats, winning awards and elections. I looked at the room for what it was and it was a room of love. I gave one last look at the man as he bravely embraced his fate, and then I walked out of the room and met with Kat, a reaper.

'What's the verdict?' she asked. I still had the envelope in my hand as I thoughtlessly stared at it. 'Send him upstairs,' I told her. 'You got it,' she cheerfully said. Then she asked, 'What's in the envelope?' I pocketed the envelope and answered, 'Atonement.'"

The bartender was taken aback by the ending of Jaydee's story. "Why didn't you send him to hell?"

"I didn't send him to hell, because I forgave him. It's not up to God to forgive man for the sins we do to each other. Forgiveness wasn't created to please God; it was created to bring peace to man. I found peace in the end, and I wanted my murderer to find peace also. It was time for me to move on."

Struck by the wisdom of Jaydee and the compassion in his decision, the bartender was left speechless, as she believed his story. But in believing his story, a terrifying thought struck her. The hair on the back of neck stood as she started to back away. "Why did you just tell me your story? Are you here because I'm going to die tonight? Do I actually kill myself?"

Jaydee gave her a beautiful smile, one that could calm the wildest of mobs and the fiercest of storms, and simply answered, "No, for tonight I am only a messenger."

"A messenger? What does your story have to do with me?"

"Life has a funny way of being kind in even the most tragic of times. The message for you comes at the ending of my story. Before leaving the old man's house, Kat handed me my next assignment, which was marked Urgent. 'Sorry for the late notice, but this death was just predicted and is going to happen down the street in a few minutes. Fucking logistics, huh?' Kat said to me before I ran out the door to meet my appointment. I ran down the street and found my next assignment standing on the street corner in the bone-chilling wind. I remember him smiling in a way only somebody in love can smile. He had a bouquet of roses and was about to call you before the truck hit him."

The bartender gasped in disbelief and fell to the linoleum floor, crying uncontrollably. In a blink of an eye, Jaydee knelt next to her and wrapped his arms around her. He reached into his breast coat pocket, pulled out a white silk handkerchief, and wiped the tears from her face.

"As he lay on the street on the frigid night, I sat next to him and asked for his story. Let me tell you, it was one of the most beautiful stories I have heard. He lived a life full of adventure and wonder, but his answers to the two questions were spectacular and I needed to hear them that night."

The bartender gained her composure between sobs and asked, "What . . . what . . . what were his answers?"

"He told me the best thing he ever did in his life was loving you. You were the greatest thing to happen to him and every second with you was his heaven on earth. For the worst thing he did . . . was leaving you. Your fiancé lived a wonderful life, and his answers were true and beautiful. I sat there with him on that cold street and comforted him as he took his final breaths. I saw Kat a block away walking toward us and went to wave at her, but your fiancé grabbed my hand and asked me to do him a favor."

"What . . ." she gasped in between sobs, "did he ask you to do?"

"He wanted me to tell you that one day you two will be together again because lovers can be lost but your love will never be; however, until you'll meet again, please live your life. He wanted you to be happy and enjoy your life. He doesn't want your story to be filled with bitterness and regret but with beauty and wonder."

The bartender cried a little more as she hugged Jaydee. "Thank you," she sobbed. "Thank you for giving me peace."

Jaydee handed her the silk handkerchief. She wiped the tears from her face, then managed to break into a smirk and said, "Your drinks are on the house," though when she looked around, she didn't see Jaydee, the bar was empty. Her encounter with Jaydee felt as if it had taken an hour, but the clock showed a minute past midnight.

Have I gone mad with grief? she thought.

She was close to dismissing the encounter as a delusion brought on the anniversary of her fiancé's death, until she looked down at the white silk handkerchief in her hand. She examined the handkerchief and found the initials J. D. embroidered into a corner of the silk cloth. The bartender smiled and tucked the handkerchief into her pocket, then quickly closed down the bar.

As she walked into the Chicago night, gentle flurries of snow danced in the air, lightly falling on her face as she stopped and looked up into the night sky. For the first time in a long time, the bartender felt joy and embraced her life again and she sung *Home* for the world to hear.

* * *

"Is that what you are, a judge?" Rick asked.

She hesitated with her answer.

"So you're telling me you were sent by God to weigh my soul because I'm dead or dying?"

She breathed for a moment, "Sort of. You're still alive, but in your case, you have a decision to make: life or death. You didn't kill yourself, but you're close to death, and this storm and the final climb to the top of the canyon is what's going to kill you. I'm here because you still have a choice. Somebody cares for you enough to send me here to listen to your story and help you make a choice."

Rick leaned his weary back against the canyon wall. "Why me?"

"Why not you, sweetie? Believe it or not, you're a good man and the world needs good men like you."

Rick stood and launched into a tirade. "I'm no one special. Do you say this because of what I did in Savannah? I'm not sure if I even did it for the right reasons. I thought I did it to help the good cops and protect the public. Now I wonder if I lied to myself to justify my revenge against the city, or if I did it for my ego because I couldn't resist taking on a whole police department, to go toe-to-toe against corruption just so I can say I did it. I'm not a good man. I'm not worth fighting for."

Rick breathed heavily, pacing back and forth. "I don't know what divine being sent you or why my subconscious may have created you, but I don't deserve it. I don't deserve to be saved. And if you are real, then why waste yourself on me? Why help me when there are fucking little boys in Africa being used as child soldiers and little girls having their genitalia mutilated? Hell, there are fucking children back home whose parents are just below garbage who need your help. Why don't you and whoever sent you go help them out and mind your own fucking business?"

Her face became stern as she charged toward him.

"How dare you say that to me!" She shoved her hands into his chest. "How dare you say that about yourself! How dare you foolishly believe that you know how and why the world really works. You know nothing. You trying to understand God is like a dog trying to understand Newton.

That's one of your faults; you're arrogant while at the same time being so self-defeating. You're a fucking walking contradiction. I was sent here not only for me to hear your story but for you to speak it. You need to hear your own story told."

"No, I'm done. I'm fucking done with the pain and torment. I don't want to hear my story. Just leave me here. Let me die."

She walked over to face him, fury in her eyes.

"Tell me your story!"

"No!"

"Tell . . . me . . . your . . . story!" she commanded between shoves.

Rick took her shoving and did not resist. "For what? So you can 'weigh' my soul? So you can judge me or some demented shit like that? You're not even fucking real. You're just a hallucin—"

She suckered punched him in the stomach. He bent over in pain. Rick had taken many hits in his life, but she punched harder than any man had or can. "Does that feel real? Now you're going to stop with this self-pity bullshit. Tell me your story so that you can finally see the man you really are!"

Rick clutched his stomach. Catching his breath, he yielded. "My name is . . ." he said between painful breaths. "My name is . . . Rick Esperanza and this is my story."

Rick's Story

I was born in New York City into a seedy and crooked family. My father was a textbook sociopath. He lied to and stole from his family, friends — anyone he spoke with for more than ten minutes.

My father had a drinking problem. He'd find a way to con people in a feeble attempt to feed his greed. We had barely any money, but his constant materialism sucked any funds we needed for rent or food into his piece-of-crap Mercury Sable or his high-end clothes. He'd try to impress people just so he could steal from or con them.

He was a charmer though. If you met him, you'd fall in love, but that was just a front. To me, what made him a monster wasn't the moments he'd lie or steal, or even the time he killed my dog because it kept barking; it was when I'd watch him beat my mother. I'd sit against the wall with my little brother as my father grabbed her by the hair and threw her against the wall, clumps of hair hanging in his hands. I felt so much shame. I wasn't strong enough to stop the beatings. I'd just sit there helpless holding my teddy bear, telling myself happy stories as I watched her bleed. I'd wish I were strong enough to stop it. I wish I could have done something to stop him. Maybe if I had my life would have turned out differently. My biggest fear was becoming him. To lie and to hurt the people I love. It's a terrible burden knowing that you were bred from a monster and that you have some of his qualities.

My mother, despite being the victim, wasn't an angel herself. She'd take her anger and frustration out on me because I was defiant, and I'd be the one to tell her and my father how wrong they were about their decisions. Both liked my brother, who'd say nothing, more, so I got accustomed to feeling unwanted, being a loner. My brother would usually take advantage of my parent's fights and their love for him by asking for better toys and clothes while making me do all the cooking and the chores.

My mother became more hostile toward me after the divorce. She'd call me names and ask why did I "have to be so weird." She'd hit me whenever I'd defended myself, but I'd never hit back, even when she came close to breaking my nose a few times. I'd find solace in school. I was an awkward outcast but loved studying and playing sports. On the weekends, I worked. Sadly, my mother would always find my money. She'd use it to buy alcohol for her and her friends.

Then one tragic day, when I was seventeen, my brother left home to live with my father. My mother and brother had gotten into an argument over my brother's laziness and failing grades. On that fateful night, he came back to grab a few more bags of his clothes and to show off his new phone and sneakers my dad had bought him, then cursed at my mother and left. I remember vividly my mother standing in the middle of my living room crying her eyes out because two men had now left her. I went to hug her, to comfort her, but she pushed me. She told me to get away. At that painful moment, I learned I wasn't loved or wanted. The one person who was supposed to love me unconditionally had just rejected me. I never felt so alone in my life. It taught me to shut people out. To keep people at a distance and never form attachments because it would be too unbearable to be rejected again by someone I loved.

My senior year of high school my mother decided to move away so that she could start a new life, to get away from her pain and sorrow. She left me with my uncle, who turned out to be a personified contradiction. I haven't seen her since. He taught me to be ethical and not to be afraid to stand up for what I believed in. He'd try to help me get past my feelings of isolation and teach me how to be critical thinker. I miss the talks we'd have at his kitchen table. We'd sit there at night and bond while he smoked his cigarettes. He'd teach me how to pick up women, how to negotiate, fix cars, and other subjects my father never taught me. I loved my uncle but he had his demons. He had anger control issues and constantly pushed away the people he loved because he had to be in control. He always had to have it his way, always thought he was right.

One day my uncle had one of his anger fits over my chores not being done on time I was working heavy hours before leaving for college. Now looking back, I can see it wasn't the chores he was upset about but his fear of losing me. My uncle asked me to sit down and began bringing up my faults and my past with my family. He started to tell me why I was going to fail in life, why I wasn't going to be accepted and wasn't going to succeed without his help.

He went on to tell me that he thought about going to buy a prostitute for me because he thought I was going to rape someone, as I was eighteen and had never had a girlfriend. I was horrified by his accusations. At the time, I was awkward and didn't have confidence in myself to ask a girl out. I was told I was handsome and charming, but I didn't want to feel attached because of my fear of rejection. His scornful statement caused me much anxiety; my biggest fear is to hurt people. I never want to bring pain into somebody's life, because I know how it feels to be let down and hurt.

My uncle kept pushing my buttons, kept tearing at scars he'd helped me heal, all in an attempt to see my reaction and to control me, to always need him. I became overwhelmed by rage and the sadness of my uncle's betrayal, so I cracked the table with my fists as I slammed them against it and screamed at him in anger. He smiled knowing that he'd solicited the response he wanted. Then he stood, walked into his room, and walked out with his revolver. He sat down back at his seat at the table, the same table where we'd have long talks over dinner and play chess, and then he pointed the gun at me. He told me he was afraid of me because of my size and he would shoot before I could hurt someone. I was mortified as I sat there, the gun pointing at me. He gave me an ultimatum: always do what he said, or fail in life.

I was terrified and heartbroken that a man I loved and respected now had a gun pointing at me because he was afraid to lose me. I sat there with the barrel of a gun pointing at my heart and made a decision: I brought my chest to the barrel, looked him in the eye, and told him to shoot. His expression of surprise said it all. I'd called his bluff. I walked out of the house and never saw him again.

I went to college in Florida, and it was a blessing for me because I felt free as I grew into my own man. I was part of a fraternity, student government, and I was even the homecoming king. I started to make friends, but I never let people get close. I always kept them at a distance and never fully trusted people with my true self. I started dating, even lost my virginity, but I never had anything that lasted. I'd go out on a few dates, but I'd find a reason to break it off, or I'd do something awkward and scare them away. I studied psychology because I wanted to know why people became who they are and know why I am the way I am, but I ended up self-diagnosing myself with depression and social anxiety disorder, primarily abandonment issues. I didn't seek help because I didn't have any medical insurance and I was afraid of the stigma of having a diagnosed mental illness. I didn't want to be looked down upon.

I knew I wanted to be in a career where I could help and protect people, so I tried to become a US Marine Corps officer. I was accepted in training but was told I wasn't good enough because I wasn't a fast runner. I tried again my senior year and put all my time and energy into passing the running test again, which I passed. Unfortunately, the Recession happened, and the Marines were not accepting any more applications for officers due to meeting quota. I was devastated because I put everything I had into becoming an officer.

Heartbroken from the Marines, I didn't know what I wanted to do after college, so I drove my piece-of-crap Ford Taurus across America. I'd no clue where I was going but kept driving and visiting famous US landmarks. My favorite of these was the Grand Canyon, where I felt an overwhelming sense of calmness and contentment. I'd never seen something so beautiful in my life; no picture in existence does the Grand Canyon justice. You have to see it to understand the majesty of it. As I stood there feeling the hot sun warm my face and watching the sparrows fly over the canyon, I made a decision to continue to help people. I decided to become a police officer.

Seven months later I was hired by the City of Savannah and sworn in as a police officer; this was the start of my downfall. I was excited to join the department but slowly started to witness the corruption of the department and the city. I witnessed cops take money from drug dealers, steal from homes that were burglarized, or order us not to arrest people because of whom that person knew or was related to. I kept my head low and kept to myself because there was none to whom to report the activity. The police chief was rumored to be protecting gang members, and the Internal Affairs investigators he handpicked were protecting the corrupt cops but punishing the good ones who made innocent mistakes. There were even rumors of good cops who attempted to make a change being forced out of the department by gang members attacking them at their homes, on the police chief's orders.

Fortunately, I was able to go unnoticed and just did my job. I helped out as many people as I could, and I fell in love with what I did. Even though it was dangerous and stressful, I felt satisfied with knowing that something I did helped somebody. I've also seen terrible things as a cop. It's horrifying to have a woman the same age as you die in your arms while her family looks at you and begs you to save her . . . no matter how bad I wanted to, I couldn't cry for her.

I was doing well for myself and was considered for the detective opening in the precinct while at the same time I had active applications in a few federal agencies and other police departments. I wanted a new life and to get away from the corruption.

During this time, I met the person I thought I would grow old with, Mal. She was a skinny, nerdy brunette from Liverpool whom I'd met on a cruise. I fell deeply in love with Mal, and for the first time in my life, I allowed someone into my heart. Our relationship grew intense, and we both admitted that we wanted to marry and grow old together, to have children, and to make a life with each other. Mal brought a smile to my face, which had been missing, and she made me feel I had everything I could want. I didn't feel alone anymore. I felt I could finally let my guard down, to actually let go of my melancholy that has haunted me my entire life, embrace a life of happiness, and look to the future with optimism.

Sadly, that all changed with Carla. I was dispatched to a house where a woman called crying hysterically for help. Half a dozen cops and I responded to a house in an upscale neighborhood, the most lavish house on the street. On the front steps sat a woman with her head cradled in her hands, covering her face. Her leg was blackened from and it looked like it was broken. I went to ask what was going on and she wouldn't lift her face to look at me. I sat down next to her and gently asked what had happened and assured her I was there to help.

The woman lifted her face, and I was mortified to see the fresh black bruises and broken eye socket. Carla then told me that her husband was in the house and that he'd been drinking. She asked why I was there because

"I wasn't going to do anything, just like the other cops." I was confused and didn't know what she meant, but I walked into the house and saw her husband sitting on the chair with a smirk on his face, drinking his whiskey. I grabbed him by the shirt and threw him onto the sofa, then started handcuffing him. He kept yelling I was making a mistake of a lifetime. Maybe I was, now looking back on it.

As I walked him outside, I saw a dozen more cops, my sergeant, and an unmarked black Tahoe. The Internal Affairs lieutenant stepped out of the back of the Tahoe, and I caught a brief glimpse of the police chief sitting inside. The lieutenant and my sergeant walked up to me. The lieutenant had another officer remove the handcuffs from Carla's husband. The lieutenant commanded me to let him go, and when I asked why, he said curtly, "Because it's an order." With concern in his voice, my sergeant told me not to make the arrest because the husband was the cousin to the police chief. The arrest, he explained, would end my career.

I stood there for a moment weighing my options: my career or helping this woman. They knew what he'd done. They knew how badly he'd beaten Carla, and he would get away with this heinous act because of the corruption and his relations. I then looked at her, tears falling from her black eyes, and I couldn't take it. I couldn't look the other way. I walked over with the shock on the lieutenant's face and admiration on my fellow cops' faces, grabbed the husband, and placed him in the back of my car and drove him to jail myself.

I was called into Internal Affairs the next day, but this time I had a voice recorder hidden on me. I was interrogated by the lieutenant and told I shouldn't have made the arrest because he was the chief's cousin; I was being placed on suspension. My heart was shattered from the betrayal of my own department. My hands trembled when I handed over my badge and gun. I put my job on the line for doing the right thing, and now I was being punished for it. At the time, I'd finally started to see a therapist because my relationship with Mal was becoming strained and my depression and anxiety were worsening. I thought it was a secret, but they were able to obtain my therapist's notes on my diagnosis of depression and social anxiety disorder. They threatened to use it against me. I told them I would fight them on this action. The lieutenant stood, leaned over his desk, and said, "I would watch your back from now on."

As I walked out of the Internal Affairs office in disgust and disgrace, I saw Carla sitting in the waiting room. Her face was worse than when I'd first seen it. Her face was completely swollen. She wore an eye patch, and her leg was in a cast. Tears ran down her eyes as she cried seeing my sorrowful expression. "I'm sorry," she whispered as I walked out the door.

I went home and contemplated what to do. I had the recordings of the lieutenant telling me I shouldn't have made the arrest because of the husband's connection, but I had no one in the department to give them to.

The people that could have made a change were either corrupt or had turned a blind eye because they were afraid to take a stand. I was afraid, terrified — not only for my career but now for my life — but I couldn't look the other way. I couldn't stand by and let someone else get hurt. I couldn't watch anymore as good cops were being scarified to protect the corrupt ones. Maybe it was the empathy I felt for victims for being one myself. Maybe I was idealistic, obsessive, and even delusional; whatever it was, I couldn't look the other way. Later that week I secretly met with a reporter and gave him copies of the investigations and the recordings. He agreed to do his own investigation but wanted to wait for the trial to publish the article.

While I was waiting for the trial, things with Mal were getting worse. She'd gone back to Liverpool for work, but I could tell she was getting more distant on the phone. I'd vent to her about what was going on with work, but it seemed as if she didn't care. Before she left, we picked out the ring, and I put a deposit down on our small wedding. I had bought a ticket to Liverpool to see her a week after the trial, but I had a feeling something bad was going to happen.

I went to trial and not surprisingly, Carla didn't show up. She left town, maybe to escape or maybe she was forced out, but the judge threw out my case stating that I'd made an improper arrest. He said there wasn't enough evidence to prove abuse. He claimed that I'd abused my power as a police officer for making the arrest. It didn't help finding out the judge and the chief were golfing buddies and related through marriage. I walked out the courthouse beaten and miserable. My reputation was muddied in the courts.

The reporter and I met again at a coffee shop close to where I lived, and he gave me a choice: print the report, which could mean the end of my career and I would be an open target, or we could bury it. We could let it be and just move on.

I was left with a heart-wrenching decision; I could turn a blind eye, try to salvage my career and possibly save my life, or I could take a stand. Try to inspire change. I told him to print the story. He told me it would be printed at the end of the week. I had already retained a lawyer just in case and had taken a few weeks off so that I could see Mal and get away from the aftermath after the article ran.

Later that night, though, I received a call from an blocked number. I could hear the faint sound of the police radio traffic in the background as the voice told me anonymously, "They know about the article. Watch your six." Then the line went quiet, replaced by the loud beating of my heart. I'd had many panic attacks in the past, but this was the worst. My chest felt as if it were going to explode. I took a few of the anxiety meds my therapist had prescribed, but it did nothing to ease the attack.

I called Mal, but we ended up getting in an argument about the decision I'd made. She told me I should have looked the other way and not have made the arrest. She chastised me for making the arrest and then started to tell me she was spending time with a man she used to date before she'd met me. She'd briefly mentioned the man before and said he was just a friend, but my jealously and distrust of the friendship had gotten the best of me. We fought about the guy and about how she'd become more distant. Mal then told me she needed to think about our relationship and hung up the phone.

I sat there that night afraid and in despair. My world was coming apart. Now I was afraid I might lose the love of my life . . . and my life. I walked over to my closet, took out my shotgun and my Glock, and sat in my leather armchair in my living room. I sat across my front door, ready for whomever might come for me.

I sat there every night, weapons in hand, until the morning of the article. I was now at the will of public opinion. The citizens might think nothing of the case, they might think I was wrong and want me fired, or they might finally have enough of the corruption and demand a change. Whatever they were to decide, my career was over. I was a whistleblower, and there was no way I was coming back from it.

I looked online throughout the day and was surprised to find that I had overwhelming support from the public who wanted a change. I was ecstatic to know my risk may have paid off . . . until the city held a press conference. I watched in horror as the mayor and the city council defended the police chief and claimed that I was a rogue cop who may have been mentally unstable. They didn't even acknowledge the recordings or the other evidence I'd supplied. The reporters asked about the other reports of corruption made and the evidence, but the mayor just said she had full faith in the police chief, then quickly exited the stage.

I sat in my apartment in shock. I couldn't feel anything. I'd gone completely numb watching my career and reputation destroyed by corruption. I sat there in silence until my phone buzzed. It was a long message from Mal. She broke up with me. My heart broke as I listened to the message; she blamed me for the break up. She called me needy, said I wasn't the man she'd thought I was. I wasn't there for her and didn't appreciate her. She then used my fears of hurting her like my father did to my mother against me. She said I was aggressive and should have trusted her more, even though she'd made me feel uncomfortable spending time with her ex-boyfriend.

I never felt so alone and so vulnerable. She used my past and my insecurities against me and made me blame myself for our failed relationship. I had tried so hard for us to be together, looking the other way when I noticed her faults, all so I wouldn't lose her. How could someone be so cold and cruel to a person she supposedly loved? I had taken the painful abuse of my family. I had people die in my arms as a cop, and I feared for my life as a whistleblower; but none of that compared to the pain she caused me. She hurt me in a way nobody could. She was the only person I let my guard down for, the only one I would have done anything for. Now I was alone.

I sat down in my armchair, looked on top of my bookshelf, and stared at the small box that held her engagement ring. I stared at it and stared at it. I lost track of time until my phone buzzed again. It was a voicemail from Internal Affairs telling me I was fired.

I didn't know why, but I couldn't feel anything. All I felt was emptiness as I walked into the kitchen, grabbed the bottle of scotch, and sat back in my armchair. I kept drinking as I stared quietly at the box. I thought drinking the entire bottle of scotch would help me feel something, but it didn't. I just stared and stared until I had the thought of us still getting back together. The thought caused my sadness, and rage rushed over me. I threw the empty bottle of scotch against the wall and began destroying my apartment. I threw picture frames of Mal and me against the wall. I took my police uniforms and my graduation pictures in the kitchen sink and lit them on fire. I tossed furniture across my apartment and punched holes in the walls.

After I was done with my blind rage, I collapsed on the floor and cried. I cried for hours. My life felt as if it were over. I rolled onto the floor, a sharp piece of picture glass stabbing me in the arm. I went to push the frame away and saw the picture of the Grand Canyon I'd taken a few years ago. In that moment, that nostalgic feeling of wonder and beauty for life at seeing the Grand Canyon, I decided to end my life there, at the canyon. I didn't want to end it at a place I despised, at a place of terrible memories and broken dreams. I wanted to end it at a place that had meaning for me. I packed a bag, my teddy bear, and my Glock, and then I took off in the Mustang, never to feel this pain again.

* * *

Rick finished his story and stared at his companion in grief.

"Is this my life? Does trouble find me or do I create it? I ask for peace but I get torment. I just want to be at peace but trouble finds me." Rick paused and watched the storm grow fierce as it approached them. "Do you know how it feels to put everything on the line? To sacrifice everything you are and have because you tried to do the right thing but found out that it doesn't matter? That what you did, what you sacrificed didn't matter. Do you know how it feels to live with the knowledge that you took a risk to help others, a risk where the people who had the power to make a change were too afraid to try, and to know that it didn't matter? Do you know how heavy that torment is? And then, the person you loved, the one you thought was your soul mate crushes the heart you gave her and leaves you when the times get tough and blames you for it?" Rick sobbed. "I . . . tried . . . I tried desperately to save our relationship. I tried desperately to save the city, but I couldn't do it . . . I wasn't good enough for them. I wasn't good enough for her."

Rick hunched over on his knees and breathed heavily from the cathartic moment.

"Is this my life? Is this what it amounted to? Constant suffering? Constantly being placed in situations where I'm forced to rebel? Will the people I love constantly hurt and abandon me? You want me to live? For what? Why endure? I just want to die and find peace from my depression! I don't want to feel the pain of knowing my career and my life is over. I don't want to think about her anymore, and I don't want this terrible heartache when she does come to mind. I don't want this life you want me to keep living."

They both went quiet, the growing rumble of thunder and rush of wind filling the silence.

"You have a destiny. You are going to do great things," she said.

"Why? I'm just some guy who tried to kill himself and failed."

"You are going to do great things, not because of humanity's version of fate. You are going to do great things because you choose to. Becoming a great person is not about chance or having some unseen entity pave the path for you. Fate is a choice. It is a difficult, frightening, and lonely choice, but a choice worthwhile. You will do great things because you choose to do the things people are afraid to do. You will do great things because you dared to be bold and venture into the unknown. You will do great things because you choose to face your demons and take a chance on yourself, even though you lack faith in who you really are. You will do these things because you choose to be brave. Humanity believes that their life is on a set path, and they accept whatever happens to them. They believe that God is in constant control of their lives, but in reality, she gave you freedom and potential. You have a choice in who you can become and whether you want to fulfill your potential or not."

"God's a woman?" Rick asked.

"It makes sense, doesn't it? Look at her mood swings called the Old Testament and the New Testament." She chuckled and smiled wryly.

"Who am I?" Rick muttered as he tried to control his sobbing.

"You are what you've strived to be your entire life. You are what you deny yourself to be. Despite what you tell yourself now, you have and will always be that person. You are a good man."

She held Rick's hand and looked him in the eye. "The world needs people like you. No, you will not be in history books and you will not be rewarded in this life. You will be judged and be misunderstood. But people like you have the highest honor among men because you will do the things people are afraid to do. You may not think it matters and goes unnoticed, but you're wrong. People are inspired. People are protected. People will look back at your kind deeds and realize they can be brave, and you will have started a contagion of compassion. Great things are accomplished by the men who realize that humanity has so much potential, the men who are willing to do what it takes to prove it.

"I know you're heartbroken, in pain, and lost. You have gone through a lot, but so have others. There are children who will never see adulthood; they were born in the wrong place, diseased, or gunned down by madmen. Be grateful you've made it this far and were able to live life. You will be made right, in time, but you will not make it if you give up. Man can destroy your accomplishments, but they cannot destroy your spirit. The gods can make your life hell, but they can never destroy your spirit. Only you can destroy yourself. Your spirit is bruised and broken but refuses to yield. You're heroic. So you must decide for yourself; is your life worth living?"

Rick brooded. "Do you know how crazy I am? Fuck, not only did I commit career suicide, but I even tried to literally kill myself. All because I couldn't walk away, I couldn't leave it alone. All because I am obsessed with fairness to the point of self-destruction. I lost my job, my future, and my love because I couldn't look the other way. That isn't a mark of a hero. That is a mark of a fucking obsessive self-righteous lunatic. I'M NO HERO!"

"Yes you are!" she screamed. "Today's heroes are glorified. They're the athletes who make millions but then beat their wives off the fields.

They're the actors celebrated for impersonating the real people who lived the lives they're portraying and, sadly, the execs behind the production exaggerating those lives being portrayed because the facts aren't profitable enough. They're the politicians who keep getting re-elected only because they pander to people's ignorance and hatred instead of their intelligence and their moral compass. You're not. You're the real deal. You'll do the right thing no matter what. No matter how bad it hurts, and no matter what the cost, even if it is your future. People like you are not celebrated, not rewarded, and most often not acknowledged, but your actions matter. The actions you take are dense and are viral. Your type help make the world a better place because you're not afraid to try."

"My type?" asked Rick.

"The unsung heroes. The soldiers who risk life and limb for the people they care about. The teachers who works in inner city schools and strive to create a future for their students. The scientists who devote their lives to expanding humanity's knowledge for the sake of enlightenment. The doctors and nurses who put up a fight to preserve a life. The politicians who make an unpopular decision because it will help others and not themselves, their donors, or their party. A single mother who would work three jobs just to let her kids have a future. And a cop who wouldn't turn a blind eye, because he believed in doing the right thing, no matter what the cost.

"You tell yourself," she continued, "that you're not a hero not out of humility but out of self-doubt and insecurity. All those years of abuse from your family and the setbacks in your career and love life have contributed to this distorted image of yourself. You think you're not good enough because you listened to the people who are little compared to you. You doubt yourself because you've reached for the things out of your reach and failed; but you went further than the people who hurt you. You're not perfect. Yes, you have an ego," she chuckled, "and you chase after the wrong women, but there's no virtue without vice."

"Why me?"

"Because who you were, and have always been, a good person. Despite all your misfortunes and suffering, you choose to be a good person instead of taking it out on the world. Instead of becoming cold and cruel, you choose to show kindness, empathy, and compassion. You do this because you know how it feels to be alone and in pain and because you wish not to cause this to others. You're not perfect, but you're a good person, a hero, because you choose to be. You dared to be better."

"What about the bullet? How come it didn't fire?"

She paused for a moment and held his hand. "You deserve a better death."

The storm grew fierce as they spoke. The setting sun had vanished. Black storms blanketed the canyon with an unnatural darkness, and its winds turned the once blazing heat into a frigid nightmare. Rick began shivered violently as he tied the tourniquet tighter around his ankle. He felt his heat exhaustion slowly turn into hypothermia.

"Please help me," he said, starting to care about his life again. "If you're here to help me, then please help me get to the top. We have to be less than a half mile away, but I don't think I can finish this with my ankle. Hell, my body feels like it's failing me. I'm dehydrated. I'm cramping all over, and I want to throw up with every step I take. Please, take me to the top."

She turned her back to Rick as she looked into the canyon. Even with the storm creating a nightmarish darkness, the canyon still looked majestic and unwavering. She was a ray of angelic light breaking the dark.

"Rick," she said with a trembling voice, the first time she had shown any type of despair to him. "This is where I leave you."

"What?" Rick braced himself against the canyon wall. "What the fuck do you mean 'This is where I leave you?' Are you going to fucking fly away or wiggle your nose and disappear into a puff of smoke? And why the hell would you leave me when I'm close to death *and* the finish line?"

Voice trembling, she breathed deeply, "I have to leave you because you have to do this on your own now. I was never here to save you. I was here to help you save yourself, and this is how far I can help you. The next half of a mile will be the most painful event in your life, as you are to fight against both your failing body and the ferocious storm. You will have to make a choice before you reach the top: life or death. I've helped you see the good parts of you, but you must choose if you still want to live, and you must do this on your own."

Rick pushed himself off the wall and painfully hopped to her. He grabbed her arm and spun her around so that they stood eye to eye and chest to chest. Rick was about to yell at her until he saw her watery eyes staring back into his.

"I have come to care for you so much." She tried to control her sobbing. "And this hurts me so much, but I have to leave you."

"Please don't. Stay with me," Rick pleaded. "You're the only person, real or imaginary, that cared this much for me."

She hugged him tightly. Rick dropped his makeshift crutch and hugged her back, wishing not to let her go. "Will I ever see you again?"

She squeezed him harder. "Depends on what you choose. You will see this face again, but it will not be me. When you do see her, take a chance and have faith in yourself."

"Are you real or a hallucination?" he whispered in her ear. Rick felt her warm tears pour down his neck where her head rested.

"You'll have to find that out on your own," she said.

"What is your name?" Rick asked.

She went quiet for a moment and whispered, "Elpis."

Before Rick could say another word, she pulled his head toward hers and passionately kissed him. Rick closed his eyes and took in the sweet moment, wishing it not to end as he felt her warmth rejuvenate him. For the first time in his life, he felt truly loved and cared for.

Rick opened his eyes to see that she was gone. He looked around. No signs of her, not even her footprints in the dusty trail, the only evidence the warm tears still on his neck. He stood there, weak and beaten, and began to tear as now he was alone again and unsure if he would ever see another living person again.

A sharp crackle of thunder broke Rick from his sorrow as the storm grew in intensity. Rick looked down the long path he'd painfully hiked and saw how far he'd come in life. He then looked forward and saw that he was almost done, but he would now have to face his mortality. He picked up his makeshift crutch and moved painfully forward into the oncoming storm.

* * *

As he hobbled ahead, the storm around him grew into a nightmarish rage. Fierce gusts threw Rick against the wall. The temperature dropped into a frigid hell. His sweat-soaked shirt harden into patches of ice in a matter of minutes. Hail pelted him, leaving fresh cuts and scrapes along his body. Darkness engulfed his path but teased him with the end still visible. His body became weaker with every step, each movement excruciating. His ankle throbbed and cracked every time he placed weight on it. His muscles locked up with painful cramps that sent a fiery, paralyzing pain throughout his body. Nausea overtook his dehydrated mouth, but the only thing it produced was painful dry heaves that left him weaker.

Rick stopped and looked forward. He was close to the end, only a quarter mile more of walking. Fighting through the pain and the violence of nature, he moved forward until a gust of hellish wind picked him off his feet and sent him over the edge.

He fell a few feet, then grabbed onto the rock. A terrible pain shot through his hand. He looked up to find his left hand had been impaled through the palm by a sharp branch. Rick screamed in agony, but his agony was muffled by a bolt of lightning that stuck the trail underneath his feet. Fear overcame his thoughts as he realized that he would die out there.

Rick screamed louder as blood gushed from his hand. He climbed a few feet more, but his injured ankle and impaled hand made it nearly impossible to move. His body became weaker and his eyelids grew heavier. Rick contemplated giving in to the darkness. He looked down to the drop hundreds of feet below, but he was already feeling the sweet relief of death. Rick had no more strength nor energy to keep moving forward. The idea of dying was better than enduring his bodily torment.

He closed his eyes as he hung a few feet from the ledge and started to drift

off into death's embrace.

Do Not Go Gentle . . .

A strange sense of relief washed over Rick as he floated into the black abyss. His pain began to fade as his life was ending, for the end felt needed. He began to let go of life, embracing the emptiness. He no longer felt his body but felt that he was one with the abyss. No more aching limbs, no more tearful eyes, no more broken heart. He savored the moment.

The moment was intoxicating, until the abyss was no longer a void but started to take shape and color in front of him. An image was produced around him. It was unfocused and blurry, like an old television receiving bad reception in a storm. Rick could make out a wall and a man hanging off it. As the image slowly cleared, he realized that the wall was the Grand Canyon and the man was he, barely hanging onto the wall.

Before Rick could speak, the image disappeared, replaced with multiple scenes from his past playing out in front of him. Scenes from his childhood, his school, work, drinking, with family, even his private moments. He saw all of his past play out in front of him at once, and to his surprise, he was able to comprehend each moment without being overwhelmed.

The good times were not the ones that stood out to him, only the bad times. All the abuse, the loneliness, and betrayals were replayed. Why was he being shown his past? Was he in hell? Was this his torture for trying to commit suicide? To relive every terrible moment and watch the good ones disappear. The bad moments were simultaneously played in front of him as he felt each pain and despair with no relief. He struggled to close his eyes but felt he had no eyelids. He tried to cry but knew he had no tear ducts. He tried to scream but had no voice. He could only feel the pain of his past.

Rick was about to surrender to his hellish fate until he noticed a common element in all the images. In the worst of times, in the times he was against the odds and full of fear, he had always rebelled. Looking past the pain, he was able to see that even in his dire moments he was his strongest. He saw himself brave and strong in the times when others would have collapsed into vices, defeated. He saw himself making his own path despite what circumstances dictated. He saw himself rage against his own doubt and insecurities and take the chance on himself. This was no longer a punishment but a lesson. Rick saw his true self for the first time and realized that no matter what had happened, no matter how dark and cold the world got, he had always found a way.

The images of the past quickly faded away, and he was now standing on someone's lawn, watching an old man sitting by himself on a porch at night. The house was a two-story brick colonial, full of life as the old man's family danced and laughed, happy to be together. It looked as if the old man had not only grandchildren but great-grandchildren running around the house. The old man did not smile, but he exuded an aura of contentment and happiness; this was a man at peace with life.

An old woman then walked out the front door and gracefully sat on the old man's lap, kissing him on the cheek and lying her head on his shoulder. She was beautiful. They were beautiful. It was love Rick saw in this image, pure love. Then the old man turned his head and looked toward Rick. He looked closer at the old man and gasped as he recognized the man. The old man was Rick. This man had become the things Rick had always wanted. A powerful positive feeling overtook his body, a feeling not felt before, one he could not name. Old Rick caressed the old woman's hair and gently kissed her on the forehead, then turning his noble gaze to Rick, said one word, "Choose."

The world went black again as he was back into the abyss. He felt at peace in the darkness, but he wasn't satisfied. Rick did not want to die like this — cold, alone, and unfulfilled. He did not want to die because the odds were against him. He did not want to die because life was against him.

Rick wanted to be the old man. Rick chose to live.

Slowly, he opened his eyes. The wild and rabid maelstrom flailed around him. He examined his hand, still impaled by the branch; his other hand was slowly losing its hold. Rick felt his body wanting to quit as the storm was working against him; yet a fiery rage was building inside him.

"I choose to live," he said hoarsely, yanking his hand from the branch, an agonizing pain shooting through his body. Rick's other hand squeezed the wall hard enough that he felt the rock crumble under his grasp. Both legs found an equal footing underneath him as he planted himself against the jagged wall. The wind wailed around him as the hail and rain barraged his body. Despite his pulsating pain and the flowing blood, his left hand shot above his right and grabbed onto the crevice above him. Using all his strength to lift himself up, he pulled himself over the edge.

Lying on his back on the now flooded and muddy path, Rick looked into the raging storm, panting deeply for air. Black clouds swirled above him. Lightning shot wildly in and around the canyon. The wind blew chunks of stone and tree off the cliff walls and across the horizon as dagger-like icicles took their places around the final part of the path. The blood around his left arm froze to his skin and to the ground. Rick looked into the eye of the maelstrom and saw only hell on earth blocking his path.

He picked himself up and stood tall through the piercing wind as a barrage of softball-sized hail fired on him. The storm's howl shook the earth beneath him, making its final attack, but Rick stood tall. Every black day, every moment of loss, and every pain in his life had no longer weakened but empowered him. No more self-loathing and doubt, only rage.

A rage brew inside of Rick, a rage so fierce that the maelstrom took notice. With every step Rick took his body begged him to quit. His injured ankle pulsated with pain. His muscles cramped to the point of locking up, and his body violently shivered to the point of a seizure, but he raged on. His body was failing him; the maelstrom wanted to end him, but he raged on because he chose life over death.

"I . . . choose . . . to . . . live," he said with every painful step forward. A gust of wind bashed him against the wall but he pushed on. His body pleaded with him to quit, while nature yearned to destroy him, but he raged forth. Every black day in his life no longer haunted him but strengthened his resolve to keep going.

"I . . . choose . . . to . . . live!" he yelled at the end of the path shortly ahead. A gust of wind lifted Rick off his feet, nearly throwing him off the cliff, but he punched the muddy path and crawled forward. Tree branches, stones, and hail pelted Rick as nature fought wildly against a force that wouldn't be stopped. Rick felt his body surge with life as he crossed the end of the path and spied the closed tourist shop.

Rick lay on his side, catching his breath, as he looked into the maelstrom eye to eye. The long path from the middle of the canyon to the end was now pitch black as the maelstrom made its final attempt on his life.

"Fuck it!" he yelled, the hard wind nearly puncturing his eardrums. Rick slowly got onto one knee, then onto the other. He painfully lifted himself off the ground and stood tall, as he was now standing on the edge of the cliff, overlooking the canyon and facing the maelstrom. It gave its final howl and its final attack, shooting a bolt of lightning toward Rick, but he did not flinch. The bolt struck down a tree near the souvenir store. No longer in fear, no longer wishing to die, feeling only a fiery will to live, Rick took a step forward as he threw his arms behind him. Baring his chest to the maelstrom, he roared, "I . . . CHOOSE . . . TO . . . LIVE!"

The storm whimpered to Rick's roar, for its fury was no match for a man's will to live. The maelstrom yielded and came to its end as he fell to his knees and stared into the sky, watching the clouds break away and freeing the moon's glow to grace the canyon. The moonlight danced across the beautiful crevice as the stars shined brightly, like the reflection of light from the dew of summer grass. Rick watched, an overwhelming joy filling his frigid, beaten body; for once in his life, he had found peace with himself and the world.

Finally, exhaustion overcame his body and he fell onto the muddy ground. Shallower and shallower, his breaths came and went. His eyelids flickered closed, as the last image he saw was the welcoming moon over the canyon, lighting the horizon for one last taste of wonder.

At the End of All Things

It was a beautiful sunny day for the Second City. The heat was slight as a cool breeze swept off Lake Michigan. The cozy Italian restaurant sat underneath the shadow of the Sears Tower, though it was blocks away.

The staff was able to relax as now the tables were filled sporadically with tourist and locals. The bartender placed an order for a deep-dish pizza and made an Old Fashioned for a man sitting at the bar who looked as if he'd been beaten to death. The man's hand was freshly bandaged, and his ankle sported a black plastic cast, but for someone who looked as if he'd been through hell, the man seemed at peace with the world.

"Here's your Old Fashioned, easy with Knob Creek Bourbon," the bartender said, serving the beaten man, then hesitating briefly "So, buddy . . ." The man glared at him with an expression older than his years. "What happened to you? Were you in an accident?"

The man's gaze passed over the bartender and into the mirror, staring into his reflection and smiling brightly. "No, I was injured doing a much needed hike in the Grand Canyon," said Rick.

"Really?" the bartender said with interest. "How was it? I've been meaning to do it, but I never seem to get the time."

"It was life changing. Just make sure you check the weather before you go," Rick said cheerfully.

The bartender smiled, then walked away to help another customer.

It was a new feeling having this positive attitude toward life. No longer did he brood and expect the worst, but now he felt balanced, as he realized that suffering is part of life, but so is good, and he felt confident to meet them both.

Rick looked at his bandaged hand. Slowly, he made a fist. The pain was only moderate this time, and it seemed to be healing faster than the doctor had predicted. Rick recalled waking up in the hospital bed three weeks prior, asking the nurse, "Did I finally die, and please tell me you're real. I can't take another mind game from a woman."

The nurse had an expression of humor and confusion, but she explained to him how fortunate he was to be alive. She told Rick how lucky he was that the park rangers found him after such a powerful storm. One of the rangers was her fiancé and had told her that he and his partner were checking on the campsites before the storm, helping campers into the nearest shelter. Both were driving to a campsite east of the souvenir shop when the worst of the storm descended and forced them to park their Jeep on the side of the road. The storm lasted an hour and both men began to fall asleep, until they were awoken by an earth-shaking thunder, followed by what they thought was an animal's roar. The storm suddenly cleared away, and they saw Rick lying on the edge of the cliff. They rushed over to him and found him unconscious on the ground. They were able to stabilize him before having him flown out to the hospital. Rick, she explained, was treated for hypothermia, his impaled hand and broken ankle, multiple abrasions across his body, dehydration, cracked ribs, and mild frostbite. The nurse said either it was dumb luck or divine intervention that her fiancé and his partner had stopped at the right place that night. Nobody was scheduled to come around that souvenir shop until the next morning. By then Rick would have been dead.

Rick waited another day in the hospital so that the nurse could introduce him to the rangers who'd saved his life. He graciously thanked them. The nurse's fiancé was a pleasant and caring man who'd seemed happy to see Rick doing well. The ranger surprised Rick saying that they'd found the keys to his Mustang in his pocket and driven it to the hospital parking lot, but that was more for the joy ride then out of pity for Rick.

Lying in bed, he watched the ranger sweetly embrace the nurse before leaving for his shift. Seeing this reminded Rick what he wanted out of life now, to love and be loved.

The next day Rick collected his clothes and checked himself out. He limped his way to the Mustang and eased his still sore body into it. He smiled as he sat behind the wheel again, listening to its engine purr. He drove back to the Monte Vista Hotel in Flagstaff and picked up his luggage, safe in storage. After having the attendant help load the luggage into the Mustang, he took his teddy bear and placed him in the passenger seat and smiled at seeing him again. Rick then drove four blocks south and then east on Route 66. At the end of the road was Chicago, and Rick had always wanted to visit Chicago.

Now he was sitting at the bar, sipping and savoring his Old Fashioned. He took out his smartphone and deleted all the pictures of Mal. While deleting the pictures a news alert popped up on his screen. "Chief of Police, Command Staff Arrested by FBI on Corruption Charges, Lieutenant Commits Suicide Before Arrest." Rick didn't bother reading the full articles; instead, he pocketed his phone. He savored a sip from his drink and decided to keep moving forward and never to look back.

Reminiscing about what had happened in the canyon, wondering if Elpis was real or a figment of his imagination, Rick reached into his pocket and pulled out the bullet. Rubbing it with his fingers and examining the rear of the bullet, he realized that it didn't matter if she were real or not, because she was real enough. He was given a second chance with a better understanding of his life. No, he didn't know what would happen, or if he would ever be a cop again, but he looked forward to his future and was no longer burdened with the past. Yes, his future was unknown, but that was a good thing because the unknown had always been kind to him.

Rick felt for the first time in his life peace and love for himself. "I guess in the end of all things there is and shall always be—" and then the door loudly shut behind him.

Home by Edward Sharpe and the Magnetic Zeros played over the speakers as Rick glanced over his back, doing a double take.

It can't be, he thought.

The auburn woman walked past him, giving Rick a familiar smile. *"You will see this face again but it won't be me,"* Rick remembered from the canyon.

"Elpis?" he said.

The woman looked exactly like her, but there was something different about this woman. She sat at the end of the bar and ordered her drink from the bartender. Rick starred in disbelief, until she looked at him with those precious hazel eyes and smiled. No longer a thought in his mind but by reflex, he eased off the stool and limped toward her. She looked at him with the smile that saved him. Both locked eyes in a fateful gaze. Rick stopped in front of her as she turned toward him.

There are moments in life where you will realize that your life is going to change for the better, that your faith is being rewarded. This was

Rick's moment.

"Hi. I'm Rick."

She gazed into his eyes and warmly said, "Hi. I'm Hope."

Poems Also Written by the Author

The Dark and Narrow Path

I walk alone on this dark and narrow path,

Not knowing where I am headed and running from where I came,

I walk alone because that's all I know,

To depend on oneself and to rely on only the unreliability of people,

I walk this dark and narrow path alone,

And I have become colder ever since I first set foot on this path,

Forgetting if I am a man or the monsters in the shadows of the forest,

I have accepted the bitterness of my resentment to the ones I once loved,

Their betrayal is the sharpest of all knives.

I walk this path alone, this dark and narrow path because it's sincerer and fairer than the world I've left.

But it still burns inside me.

I push it down, I try to forget, and tell myself how foolish I am for still holding onto it,

But inside us all, even the broken ones, is hope.

I cannot deny its loving glow on this dark and narrow path;

No matter how black this path has become, its glow has also shined through,

No matter how dim it has gotten, hope has never been snuffed out.

Now is the time to walk back into the light,

To forgive the lands I left behind,

And to live for my dreams,

Because in the end there is and shall always be hope.

The Storm

I lay naked-soul on the whitest sands with clearest of water crashing at my feet. The sun kisses my skin and warms my spirit. The crashing waves bring me peace.

The rolling, rumbling sound of thunder is heard in the closing distance. I look up to see the grays of clouds slowly overtake the sun. The cool, salty wind grows strong and wraps my naked body.

The gentle drizzle dances across my holy shore and kisses my bare chest and face.

The storm is coming; I do not fear her but adore her.

I will know no loss for she brings me all.

Sunglasses

I pick up the sunglasses on my dashboard and put them on so she doesn't
see my eyes.

I hold her in my arms one last time and as we say good-bye.

The hard truth of us possibly never seeing each other again overwhelmed
me but I wear my sunglasses so she doesn't see my eyes, not wanting her
to see me at my weakest but I lie to myself and say she was just a fling.

I walked her to her gate and gave her the last kiss we'll ever have but I
fake a smile and put on my charm to hide the pain.

Finally understanding what Sam Smith had sung about,

I sat back in my car and kept the sunglasses on to hide my eyes from the
world.

I looked in the mirror; the sunglasses may hide my eyes from the world,
from her and from myself, but it doesn't hide the tears rolling down my
cheek.

Lubec

There is a town called Lubec that lies as the eastern most town of the United States.

There is a lighthouse in this town you must go to, for it is the most eastern point of the most eastern town of the United States.

You must go there before the dawn breaks, for the solace of your soul.

At the eastern part of the lighthouse there is a smooth granite slab in the ground, you must stand on that hallowed step.

The skies will dance to the waking light, as they turn lovely oranges and rosy reds.

You will watch the clouds gently float in the air as if they were lightly brushed there by the unknown artist.

You will hear the ocean gently break against the shores and the morning birds greet the nightly owls.

You will feel the cold morning air kiss and rejuvenate your body.

You will stand on this hallowed step and be inspired by wonder and majestic of the sun rising over the horizon of possibilities.

The warmth will rejuvenate your very soul and the sun's light will reflect off the water as if it is showing you a path.

You will dance as a joyous child and sing your song for heaven to hear.

For this is a path, a path to where hope and love live again.

You must go to this town of Lubec, the eastern most town of the United

States to find profound proof that life is beautiful and where hope prevails.

Who am I?

I am who I am

And I have done what I've done

I've done bad things

But I have done good things

Am I a good man?

That is for history to decide

But I've tried to do everything I can to be one

Que sera, sera

The Fear

"I'm afraid of the monsters," the child quietly said in between her sobbing.

"Little Miss," said the comforting old man. "Yes, there are monsters in the world. They can be horrifying, cruel, and evil, but do not be afraid, because for where there are monsters there are also heroes. Heroes come in different shapes and sizes; some are big and strong while others are small and fast. They may be different but they all share one trait; they choose to be brave. They choose to be brave and fight the monsters when others give into the fear. Do you know what the amazing thing is about heroes? Anyone can be a hero. You just have to choose to be brave."

Red

My heart beats faster for every step I take closer to her.

She waits in the distance for me as only a true love would.

My cheeks hurt from the smile she puts on my face.

"Hello, baby." The greeting she misses.

I slowly caress her curves, feeling her smooth skin underneath my eager

fingertip.

Her face glows red and she trembles upon my touch.

The world may judge her beauty but to me she is perfect.

She has her scars and I have mine.

She is mine and I am hers.

She waits for my embrace but I deny her for a moment; for in that moment

she tells me with her eyes how much she wants me.

Too long we have waited for each other; I no longer deny her.

We are together again, for I am hers and she is mine.

The question I must ask her.

The question I have waited to ask her since the last good-bye.

Her answer would make our love eternal.

A love that stories would be told from.

"Shall we go on an adventure?"

She gently holds my hands and smiles.

Her answer is perfect.

She is perfect.

We walk into the unknown, together.

The Unknown

Into the unknown.

Into the unknown we shall seek.

Into the unknown we shall find.

Into the unknown.

Where the restless wanderer finds a home.

Where brave men find solace.

Where the curious find bliss.

Where a hero finds his reward.

Where the close-minded do not venture.

I do not fear her for the unknown has always been kind to me.

Into the unknown.

The Sparrow

I look off unto the setting sun, watching the sky turn majestic purples and lovely oranges. I lean across the rail as we sail against the headwinds and watch the sun and sea embrace before the night comes. I watch this beautiful kiss until I see the Sparrow flying across from me. It has been days since we have seen land, so the Sparrow is our little stowaway from our last port.

I watch the sparrow fly against that strong headwind, furiously flapping its wings but able to match the wind. I wonder if she made a choice to explore. Did she choose to leave it all behind: her nest, her flock, and her life so she can set sail to places unknown? Did she choose her own freedom? If she did make that choice then I admire her. I envy her bravery. She tirelessly flies against the wind. I hold out my arm so she can land and rest on it. She turns her head and sees it but she keeps flying against the wind. I wonder if she knows that tomorrow we will dock into a place both foreign to us. What lies ahead of us both, I know not; but she knows no fear, and so must I.

The Road

You are my lover.

You are my dearest friend.

You call my name.

Who am I to deny you?

Your curves, your long winding curves, excite me.

An adventure waits as you take me where I need to be.

For I am an adventurer and you always satisfy me.

You never bore me.

You never wrong me.

You never leave me.

Fathers have left me.

Friends forsake me.

Flames extinguish in the darkest moments.

But, you have always shown me kindness.

You never leave me wanting.

You are the mystery worth solving.

The Fury of the Storm

I hide from it but trouble finds me.

You think this is out of cowardice; you are sadly mistaken.

Yes, I am afraid but not of you.

I beg for peace.

I ask this for your welfare.

You see my age, my kindness, and my compassion as weaknesses.

Your hubris wrongs you.

Your ignorance of my nature will be your downfall.

But you came knocking and I now must answer.

I am a storm.

I am fury.

I am a force of nature.

There will be no shelter.

There will be no safe quarters.

There will be no sanctuary.

For I am the storm.

Joe

A man can have hundreds of friends but none will equal to Joe,

For he is a friend like no other,

In our generation people have forgotten the worth and warmth of loyalty,

To have a friend at the end of all things is more splendid than any jewel in

existence.

Oh, to have a friend in the brightest of days and the roughest of storms!

I have had friends, who I treated as family,

But how quickly they disappeared when trouble entered,

Like the light flickered off when my day became black.

But never have I felt like that with Joe.

I must have done something right to earn the friendship of a man who

embodies the noble qualities lacking in today's world.

I am blessed to be his friend.

Oh, to have a friend like Joe!

What have I done right to deserve a friend like he?

The world can be cruel and unforgiving. Life can sometimes be

insurmountable but to have a friend like he at your side can make it feel all

the worthwhile.

And when the world beat me to my knees and I was left with nothing but

my fears and tears, I had Joe and that was all I needed.

I wish to you all that you will have a friend like Joe.

There Can Be

There can be grace in struggle.

There can be glory in enduring.

There can be fulfillment in wanting.

There can be belief in the cynical.

There can be enlightenment in failure.

There can be reason in madness.

There can be beauty in words.

There can be power in compassion.

There can be magic in love.

There is meaning in it all.

To live, to laugh, to cry, to answer the question, "why?"

At Last

I have never been in love for if I had then I would have been your man.

I search every day hoping for one night to have your head dreaming on my chest.

I may be a fool, a glutton for punishment 'cause I keep asking them, all in the hope it would be you.

To dance with you until the end.

I fear of dying before finding you. I have done many things but to love another more than myself, I have not.

Life can be unfair but I have been fortunate to live the life I lived.

But is it selfish to ask, can I just love you?

Can I be your champion?

Am I a fool because of the idea of you?

Do you exist?

Am I delusional for believing in you?

She exists! She exists! She exists!

You exist! You exist because I exist.

Integrity

I've been going around this all wrong.

I've been trying to live my life as a sane man.

To go along with how things are.

To be normal . . . how boring!

I should have just been me.

The times when I was mad was when I was the happiest.

When I didn't care what others thought.

Didn't put much thought into tomorrow because I choose to live my life,

my way.

Lovers Lost

I understand how the loveless feel when they sleep with a stranger.

Sleeping in the warmth of another person is heaven for the lost.

To feel her soft skin against mine is worth the pain in the morning.

Her smooth legs wrap around mine with her head lying on my heart keeps

me from searching for the night;

She is not mine and never will be,

For tonight her body is mine but not her heart.

Tomorrow she will be gone and I will carry on, like I have and always will,

But for tonight, I will not long for another.

Made in USA - Kendallville, IN
1181801_9781090233783